THE
WENTWORTH
TRIPLETS
MYSTERY SERIES

VOLUME 2

THE CASE OF THE BUNGLING BOAT

THE CASE OF THE STOLEN SISTER

JOANN KLUSMEYER

innovo
PUBLISHING

Published by Innovo Publishing, LLC
www.innovopublishing.com
1-888-546-2111

Providing Full-Service Publishing Services for Christian Authors, Artists &
Ministries: Books, eBooks, Audiobooks, Music, Screenplays, Film & Curricula

**THE WENTWORTH TRIPLETS
MYSTERY SERIES
FOR YOUNG TEENS**

VOLUME 2

**THE CASE OF THE BUNGLING BOAT
&
THE CASE OF THE STOLEN SISTER**

ISBN: 978-1-61314-655-2

Cover Design & Interior Layout: Innovo Publishing, LLC

Printed in the United States of America
U.S. Printing History
First Edition: 2021

Has God called you to create a Christian book, ebook, audiobook, music album,
screenplay, film, or curricula? If so, visit the ChristianPublishingPortal.com to
learn how to accomplish your calling with excellence. Learn to do everything
yourself, or hire trusted Christian Experts from our Marketplace to help.

CONTENTS

A NOTE FROM THE PUBLISHER

Although the Wentworth triplets are fictional, the models depicting them on the back cover are real triplets (Aden, Cole & Eva Claire) who, at the time, were the same age as the characters. Just like the fictional Wentworths, the real triplets and their parents are believers. And if that wasn't coincidence enough, the real dad is a world-traveling pilot just like his fictional counterpart. Interestingly, the author didn't know the models or their family. What are the odds? At Innovo we like to say, "With God—one hundred percent!"

THE CASE OF THE BUNGLING BOAT

I t was a rare October day for the Wentworth triplets. Ordinarily, they would be going to school with the others of Branson, Missouri, but instead, they had packed their African equipment for what would be a safari, but was, instead, a business trip.

Their father was a nature photographer, and this was the time to film another adventure along a riverbank. This was the time of the year that the river was not in flood stage and was not drying up. Right now, it was just right, so they were excused from attendance. Missed lessons, of course, must still be made up.

Surprisingly, their cousin Sally Copelan was also excused from school. This seemed like a one-of-a-kind experience, and her parents agreed to let her go.

The small jet lifted off the runway in Springfield, Missouri, and traveled through the clouds across the ocean. When they landed, the African sun was climbing into the sky, promising another steamy, hot day.

Immediately, they were transported to the scene of the first shooting.

Dennis Wentworth and his brother, Danny, both thirteen, watched the flowing brown water of the Senegal River as it rolled toward the ocean. Darla, the third member of the thirteen-year-old triplets, and their twelve-year-old cousin, Sally Copelan, were spraying insect repellant on the thin sleeves of their shirts and on the fine mesquite netting they would wear draped over their hats to protect their faces.

The hungry mosquitoes hovered around the water's edge in black, buzzing swarms with the noise of a million miniature helicopters, eager for their feast of human blood.

"Right now, I'm not sure Dad did us a favor when he let us cut school for this trip," Darla commented. "But he said it would be educational."

"It is. I've learned something already."

"What?"

"I didn't know until now that I hated mosquitoes so much."

Nature Photographer, Montgomery Wentworth, the triplet's father, cleaned and polished his camera lenses and examined his equipment. He repacked the equipment he had used yesterday and had it ready to put aboard.

It was time to continue filming the Senegal River of West Africa and the creatures that depended on the water flowing in it.

At the large African town of Keyes, they waited for the arrival of the river tug and its barges which would carry them down river, all the way to the Atlantic Ocean, where their own small jet plane waited to return them to America.

"I see it," yelled Dennis. "Here comes the tug. See that black speck? I'll bet anything that's it."

"Hey, Dad, it's coming!" agreed Danny.

"You girls better get on down here. Hey, Dad! Come on!"

The photographer continued to clean his camera lens. The girls ran to the pier.

"Aw, it's still an hour away."

"I'll bet it isn't."

"And then when it gets here, they'll have to unload everything that's on it before it goes back down stream."

"No, it'll just unhook the barges it brought up stream and hook onto the ones going down."

"Yeah, and that won't take twenty minutes."

"Maybe thirty minutes."

"But look," Sally pointed out. "There are still two barges with nothing on them. See, they're hooked onto ours."

"Wonder what goes on them?"

"Probably we're going to stop somewhere for something. Ask Dad."

"Dad, what goes on those two barges on the end?"

"How would Dad know? He's been busy all morning, doing stuff to the camera."

"I wanted our barges to be on the end. That way we would be on the front of the line going downstream."

"There's just one thing I wonder," Sally said.

"What?"

"Will we be going faster than a mosquito can fly?"

"Hey, Dad, how fast can a mosquito fly?"

"I know," offered Darla.

"No you don't. Nobody does."

"Yes, I do," she insisted.

"How fast, then?"

With a smug smile, she answered, "Just as fast as it has to to keep up with us."

"See, you didn't know. Nobody does."

"No, wait. They won't have to fly. They'll just rest on the barge."

"No, we'll just get new ones from the bank as we go along."

"Yeah, after we've fed these, why should they bother to go along?"

"I've fed more than my share."

"Me, too. I wish the tug would hurry."

The noisy, smoking engine on the tug was much bigger than a speck by now and was growing fast. The pier at Keyes, Africa, became a buzz of human activity as shippers checked and rechecked the safety of the goods they were shipping down river, and merchants from Keyes awaited the arrival of their goods being brought upstream to them.

The tug whistled its arrival in a long, low blast. Another tug behind it also signaled its presence.

"Look! There's two of them!"

"Sure. They like to travel in pairs," Dennis remembered.

"So they can help each other if they have trouble."

"And because it takes two tugs to get the barges back up the rapids. Going down is fast and easy, but it takes a lot of strength to fight the current in the narrows. They unhook one and tie up its barges while they get one string upstream. Then both tugs go back to get the other string."

"How do you know that?"

"I'm just smart."

"Fat chance of that."

"Wangteya told him."

"Oh."

Wangteya was the native guide they had picked up at the beginning of the river expedition, as they were filming the upper part of the river. He would go with them until they reached the ocean. Wangteya was a very big help because his English was much better than their African and this was his home country so he could answer a lot of questions.

Wangteya, who had been crouched on his heels watching the photographer, suddenly got up and walked away. He walked over to a number of carriers who were bringing crate after heavy crate down to the pier to be loaded onto the remaining empty barge. He talked with the men for a minute, then came back.

"Books," he told them. "Crates of valuable books headed for a village about sixty miles down stream."

"Books written in African?" Darla asked.

"No, English," Wangteya answered.

"But..."

"They're for a school teacher to open a school in a village."

"Oh, probably a white missionary school. Is that it?"

"No," Wangteya answered. "The carriers say not. They say African teacher coming home to teach. The village children will learn English, and then they will be able to study the books written in English."

"But, Wangteya, isn't that strange? Why would a village in Africa need to learn English lessons?"

"Not so strange if what is going to be taught is in English. Easier to teach English to small children than to change the language in the books to African."

"But why would they even want to know what is in the English books?"

Wangteya shook his head. "Is not to know, yet. Teacher will come and tell us, maybe. I could think of one reason. Many books he brings, but America had so many more than he can bring. If he teach English, then his pupils can read any book they can get, that is worded in English."

Darla nodded. "Of course. That way the pupils could even come to America and already know the language. And they could teach their own children some day."

The chuggity-chug of the powerful tug motor was loud, now, as it nudged its heavily loaded barges toward the bank. The whistle screamed in a shrill, deafening signal to the pier that they were coming in. The sound had hardly died away when the second tug sounded its own piercing whistle, announcing its own intentions.

"Here it is, Dad," Danny warned, but when he turned to look behind him, his father was gone.

"Dad?"

"He's over there, see?" Dennis pointed. And there stood the photographer aiming the camera. The object of the film was the silvery blue African kingfisher, diving like a blue feathered bomber toward the water of the river.

As the bird sliced through the surface of the water, a silver spray arose into the air to sparkle in the sun. A split second later the water parted again. The bird struggled to lift off the surface of the water with a large, flopping fish in its beak.

The weight of the fish was almost too much for the bird, and its powerful wings struggled fiercely, barely skimming across the surface of the river.

The boys eased into position behind their father, watching as the camera made a movie star of the bird. Finally, the powerful wings were able to lift off the water and circle into the sky.

"Look, Dad," Dennis pointed beside him.

A dragon fly, flitting its blue tissue-paper wings, had settled on the wet soil beside the river. Its proboscis was plunged into the mud. In addition to the water, the mud contained minerals the insect needed. And now its visit was recorded on film.

The photographer turned in a circle to make a panoramic sweep of the pier, the tug, and the string of loaded barges.

"Yeah, Dad, that's a good idea. If we make a film of all the uses of the Senegal river, the people and the tug would be a part of it, huh?" Dennis realized.

"Dad, how about those little boys?" Danny pointed out a pair of small Africans wading in the edge of the water, carrying a small, hand-made net.

The photographer turned and aimed the camera at the boys. They drew their net through the water, then laughed with glee as they realized they had actually caught a small fish in their net.

One of the boys reached into the net for the fish but it flopped out of his hand, squirting up into the air. The body of the fish glinted silver in the sun as it turned over and over above him.

The other boy caught the fish as it fell, but a flip of the powerful tail set the fish free again. The boys stared for a moment at the spot on the water where the fish had disappeared with a small splash, then they resumed their fishing efforts by dragging their net through the water.

From the pier Sally called, "Hey, Uncle Monty, come look." She pointed to a young woman approaching the riverbank carrying a small baby.

As his camera followed her, the woman waded into the water and lowered the naked baby into the water. The little fellow squealed with pleasure and splashed water with his hands, and his mother laughed with him. She rubbed his arms and legs to clean them, and then washed his hair while he squirmed and tried to push her hands away.

The mother and baby had become movie stars and their pleasure in the water of the river would be enjoyed by many people.

The tug had now released the string of loaded barges it had pulled up river and had attached itself to those returning downstream. They had spent most of the afternoon getting ready to make the trip back down river, and the sun was low as the photographer was allowed to board.

The barges were attached in pairs, side by side, and there were five pairs. Each flat-bottomed boat was about the size of a small bedroom, and they were piled so high with merchandise that when the children stood on their own barge, they could not even see the tug, almost 100 feet away.

Boxes and crates were stacked around the edges of the barges, tied and chained to hooks in the floor to secure them, and creating hollow square "rooms" inside. The "rooms" were only large enough to accommodate two, maybe three, closely spaced sleeping bags.

They were well underway when darkness fell and the sleeping bags were opened. It was totally dark when the tug was tied up to a large tree.

There was no bedtime hot chocolate, but evening devotions were held as usual. Each of the five persons would remember a Bible verse he had learned and would explain why he chose that one.

"Who wants to be first with the verse?" invited Dad.

"I do, Dad. If I don't go first, someone might get my verse. It goes, 'Study to show yourself approved.' I think that means to study so you learn how to get along in life."

His father nodded, "That would be one explanation. Next? Sally?"

"I'm ready. 'Men love darkness rather than light because their deeds are evil.' I think people believe God cannot see well at night, so they can get away with more sin."

"Like burglary?" suggested Darla.

"Yes, but God made the dark, so, of course, He can see perfectly well in it."

"All right. Danny?"

"'The fear of the Lord is the beginning of wisdom.' I think that means we can't be truly smart unless we know God first."

"Fine. Now, Darla?"

"Dad, I need my Bible. I can't think of a verse."

"Sure you can, Kitten. Think harder. We memorize verses so we'll have them with us when we don't have the Bible in our hands."

"All right, Dad, but the only one I can think of is going to sound funny. Jesus said, 'Let down your nets on the right side.' I think the disciples had been fishing from the wrong side of the boat."

"Or the left side," offered Sally.

"Maybe that was it, but when they obeyed, they caught a lot of fish."

"That was a good one. Jesus also said, 'I am the way, the truth and the light.' That is how we can be sure we are going the right way. Staying close to Him lets us always stay in His light."

Before first morning light, the tug and the barges had untied and were on their downstream trip. The tug was positioned at the rear of the ten barges, guiding and pushing when the river current was weak, and holding back when the current swept them faster than would be safe.

As it seemed, there was only one passenger on the barge besides the photographer and his family. The family occupied barges seven and eight, and the other passenger, the school teacher, was on barge nine with a lot of his books. The rest of the books were on barge ten.

One hollow square was assigned to the girls, and the adjoining one was for the boys and their dad.

Slowly at first, then faster, they moved, creating a small wake at the edges of the flat boats. The girls sat on water storage cans watching the scenery on the banks. Sure enough, there were fewer mosquitoes now, and the air was a little cooler. Not much, though.

Wangteya sat near their teacher neighbor and chatted in English.

"Name Wangteya. Crates of books for a school?"

"Name Lubo. I hope it will be a school," came the answer. "My grandfather, a tribal chief, wished me to learn good agricultural methods so he sends me to America, to learn lessons so we will not be hungry. I learn other things and want to teach. We may both get what we want."

Dennis edged closer to the front pair of barges.

"Do you have books for all grades?"

The young African nodded. "All grades will be needed if I get my way."

"Why wouldn't you get your way if your grandfather is the chief?"

Lubo smiled. "Having one thing does not mean I will get the other."

"Why not?" insisted Dennis, edging closer.

"Many reasons. My father, the chief's son, also had wishes to change things, and he is now gone."

"But won't he be back?"

Lubo shook his head. He raised his hand as though he held a spear. He plunged the "spear" forward and repeated, "Gone."

"Oh," nodded Wangteya, knowingly.

"But why?" Dennis insisted.

His father who had been listening called to Dennis. "Hush up, son. You ask too many questions."

Lubo looked across to the photographer and explained, "Is all right. My father's death was long ago. He was killed after disagreement with medicine man."

"Did the medicine man kill him?"

"Yes and no. It was a hunting accident but all the hunters were killed. Poison arrows from an enemy. No one left to say what happened."

"No eyewitness, huh?"

"No eyes still alive," Lubo nodded, sadly. "That is no eyes that would tell the truth."

Wangteya had been listening silently. "Lubo?"

"Yes, friend?"

"Medicine man, does he still live?"

Lubo nodded and turned away to look down river toward his village, as though the very words would be painful if he spoke them.

"How far away is your village?" Danny asked.

Lubo turned to look at him. "Two night stops. Third day the river goes near my village."

"How will you get these crates off?"

"The chief will have carriers waiting."

"What is the name of your village?"

"It has two names. First is hard to say the name, but it means half-hidden place."

"Is it half-hidden?"

"There was a time, yes. But now it is many huts, and trees have been cut. Not hidden now, so the new name was needed."

"What is the new name?"

"Long words hard to say, but means Pleasant Sun. Trees gone, more sun shines there."

Danny had now joined Dennis, and they both sat on the edge of their barge, dangling their feet over the edge.

"May we come over to your barge?" Danny asked.

"Boys," their father interrupted. "Don't ask so many questions. Lubo may be tired from his flight from America."

"Oh, no," insisted Lubo. "Very much awake from nerves. Company would be enjoyed by me. Young men would be a pleasure."

"Yipee!" yelled Danny as he backed up a few steps and took a flying leap across the eight feet of water that separated the barges, landing luckily on the platform beside Wangteya. Dennis was not far behind.

"Hey, Dad," Danny called, "Toss me the little camera and I can take a picture of you taking pictures."

"Here it comes."

There were thirty-seven huts clustered close together in the African village of Pleasant Sun. All around the central cluster of huts there were many more, located under the groves of trees and down toward the big river, and all together they created a large settlement.

The old chieftain of the village of Pleasant Sun was very tired. He had been unable to sleep for the last two nights, and he had walked around in the village making plans.

The barge would be bringing something that would be a great pleasure to him. It would be the homecoming of the grandson that he loved. He would be bringing the many books that had been bought with hard earned money. Books that would be so valuable for the children. Books that would teach them to grow food so there would be no more hungry years.

"The learning place will be large so my grandson will have to have much room. When he takes a wife he will have many sons and they will all know about the ways of growing food so there will never be hunger." The chief knew these words so well because he had told them to himself so many times.

Then he went on, "Other villages will hear that we have no hunger and they will come to learn our secret. We will tell them gladly.

"If there is no hunger, why would there be any war? My grandson, the new chief, will tell them everything. They will bring their small boys to learn the secret of no hunger. This is what will happen because I have decided it." The old man nodded with satisfaction and then continued.

"While the sons learn the secret of no-hunger, they will learn the secret of magic words that hid in what my grandson called text books. That is what he hopes."

There was another person in the village who could not sleep. He sat in his hut thinking his own thoughts. He shook his head sadly because he really liked the old chief and was sorry for what must be done. The simple fact was that the village could have gone on just like it was, and there would be no trouble but, no, the old chief thought he had to change things.

The chief should be content to rule the village and let the medicine man tell the people what they needed to know. If the chief had not been so stubborn about this, his son would also be alive today.

It could be that the grandson will bring information that would make others as smart as the medicine man, and maybe smarter. If the whole village is as smart as the medicine man, then he will have no power over them. If he has no power, then what reason does he have to live? None, of course!

And now, here comes the grandson with words that would win the people away from him, their very own medicine man. The chief should have listened when he told him that no good would come of sending his only grandson off to America.

In fact, he had told the old man that a foreign devil would attack the boy and keep him from coming home. All the village heard about this and were now saying that the chief's grandson was stronger than the foreign devil, for was he not on his way home right now?

The old medicine man shook his head, sadly. He, himself, would have no power over the people when the grandson arrived. But, of course, the grandson was not going to arrive.

It was sad, but necessary, for the sake of the villagers. A medicine man must not ever be shown to be wrong, or who would believe what he said?

The medicine man sat in his hut and watched the chief as he stood in the moonlight, staring in the direction of the big river. He would be thinking of his grandson, soon to arrive.

The medicine man, watching the motionless chief, had a thought, *Right now it must be happening. Yes, right now was the time.*

The sun sank below the tall trees that bordered the river, and the tugboat captain looked for a suitable place to tie up for the night. It was dangerous to travel at night due to snags and sandbars in the river.

Also, there was the possibility of hippos lounging in the shallows and they could cause damage. It was rare for the animals to be in the river at night. That was when they usually went ashore to graze because it was cooler at night and there were fewer other animals about. For all his fierce and powerful look, the hippo has very thin skin and can even get sunburned.

The captain of the tug selected a grove of large trees that overhung the water. The tugs were securely tied to the trees, and the barges rocked gently, clanging their chains and grating against the strong clamps that held them together.

Wangteya had decided to spend the night on the barge of the chief's son as they chatted in English about the plans for the grandfather's village. There had been a problem in Africa that may now be corrected by what was happening in the boat. Or at least, it was a start.

These two men came from tribes that spoke very different languages, but they could understand each other well when they used their English. This was a magic act that could be increased, and the more men who could talk together, the more men who would be friends. Would that not happen?

Dennis and Danny were invited to stay, but Danny preferred the mosquito net tent on the barge with his father. So after their evening devotions, Dennis leaped back to the end barge.

The three talked far into the night, but finally stretched out on the floor of the barge and went to sleep.

Quietly, carefully, five pairs of feet crept along the jungle path, being carefully mindful not to step on poison snakes.

The moon filtered through the tree limbs as the five men crept along, hurrying, yet making certain they were not seen. From the time they learned to walk, they had been trained to take steps that made no noise and it had been one of the most important lessons for young boys to learn.

They reached the edge of the water, its ripples shimmering in the moonlight. They looked up at the moon, dismayed at its brightness. A skinny sliver of a moon would be better, and no moon at all would be the best. However, moon or no moon, the job must be done tonight.

All was quiet on the tugboat, but, of course, there would be someone on watch somewhere in the tugs. That was why it was so necessary to be silent and invisible.

On hands and knees, like jungle animals, they made their way along the riverbank. Past the produce barges, small caged animals and passengers, they moved, looking carefully at each barge. They passed the mosquito net tents and took a long look at the barge on the end.

White-toothed smiles appeared as they nudged each other. It would be easier than they had thought.

On hands and knees, they approached the black water. Hardly causing a ripple, they entered the water, paddling gently under the shiny surface out to the last pair of flat boats.

Under the water they moved along until they located the heavy clasp that held the last pair of barges to the sting. The metal of the clasp was rusty and hard to move. The current had pulled at the boats until they strained in their clamps, making it necessary for the pair to be pushed a little way upstream so the clamps could be separated. Difficult, but, of course, that was why there were five men for this job.

Five dark bodies swam through the black water to the rear of the moonlit barge. One member of the four swimmers was able to get footing against a stone, and the other three paddled with silent strokes. The barge was eased backward against the gentle current for a few inches and one clamp was separated.

The swimmers silently broke their heads above the water, gulped air, and swam to the other barge, repeating the maneuver.

Quickly, then, to avoid being overran by the barges, the five swimmers dropped deep into the water and swam for the shore.

They arose silently from the water and climbed quickly up the bank and into the edge of the jungle. As soon as they were out of sight of the river, they turned and peered through the leafy jungle screen to watch the result of their handiwork.

Sure enough, the pair of cargo boats at the end of the string began to ease away, pushed gently by the current, and they separated themselves from the rest of the barges. They drifted slowly with the river current, carrying their three sleeping passengers downstream.

There were more white-toothed smiles as the five swimmers congratulated themselves on a job well done. They turned to go back to the village, satisfied that their work was completed, when a loud "CLANG" of chains and the noise of toppling wooden crates stopped them.

Barge number ten had stopped suddenly, jerking so sharply that the moonlit water rippled in every direction. Number nine barge also jerked, and the safety chain which ran from the first to the last of the string of barges caused number eight to tremble, and number seven to shiver. Everyone was instantly awake.

Lights came on and there were calls from the tug and from the shore. Men in small boats came rowing rapidly to the errant barges, numbers nine and ten.

As soon as the photographer knew Dennis was safe, he loaded the camera for low-light, and began to run the film. Up river and down, in the bushes along the bank and even in the air. He climbed up on the piled luggage to get a better view.

By that time, the owners of the tugboat had swarmed over number nine and number ten barges, now rocking at the end of their safety chain tether.

Wangteya listened to the shouted conversation. "Hitching clamps separated but safety chains held."

He listened a while longer, frowning with lack of understanding. "Strange that two clamps separated at same time. Strange to make men wonder, but no hitch is broken." Somehow, it didn't make sense to him.

More shouts were exchanged. Men dived into the dark water, then came up sputtering and shouting, only to gulp air and go under again.

Danny, Darla, and Sally stood looking down into the water, then to the straying number ten barge with Dennis aboard. If it had not been for the safety chain, he would now be far downstream.

"Dad," Darla began. "Can you make Dennis come back here?"

Danny butted in, "But it's all over now. No use for him to come here. I wish I was over there." With that statement, he began to take off his shirt to go into the water.

"No, Danny," yelled Sally at her cousin. "Don't go in there!"

His dad agreed. "No, Son. You would be in the way of the workers. They have enough trouble trying to work in the dark the way they are."

"But, Dad, I want to help."

"I said no."

"Aw, Dad..."

Then Darla pointed, "Look, Dad, Dennis is going in."

At that moment the guide, Wangteya, had eased off the barge into the water with Dennis right behind him.

"DENNIS!" But his father's call was too late. Dennis was beneath the water of the Senegal River, with who knows what kind of danger down there with him.

"Now, what did he do that for?"

"I think he wanted to help them fix it."

"No, he's just being nosey."

"But he can't see anything down there."

"He'll find that out."

"Maybe he'll find a crocodile first."

"Or a crocodile might find him."

"Do crocodiles hunt at night, Dad?"

Darla decided for herself. "No, they are cold blooded and can't move around very well at night. They need the sun to warm themselves up."

"Are you sure?"

"I think so."

"Dad?"

"Son, I don't think there is a danger from crocodiles because of all the commotion. Still...."

At that moment, Dennis popped up from the water for a breath.

"DENNIS!"

"Yeah, Dad?" Dennis sputtered.

"Get up here with me this minute."

"Sure, Dad." Dennis crawled, soaking wet, out of the water. He shivered and wrapped a blanket around his shoulders.

"Brrrr..." he complained.

"Did you see anything down there?" Danny asked. "Dad wouldn't let me in."

"Yeah, what did you see," Sally asked.

"Water, men, chains."

"I mean, what happened?"

"Nothing. Just a couple of clamps came apart."

"Came apart?"

"Yeah, but nothing got broke."

"Then what happened?"

"I told you. The clamps came apart."

Number ten barge was now slowly moving toward them, encouraged by many hands. With a lot of shouts and much diving, the clamps were refastened and number ten barge again bobbed peacefully in the water, firmly attached to its fellows. Within minutes, number nine was also solidly reclamped, and riding the ripples alongside.

It was an hour or more before the men of the tugboat crew were satisfied that everything was now safe enough to turn out the floodlights and go back to sleep.

Wangteya kept stroking his chin and muttering, "Two clamps came undone? Strange! One clamp come apart...maybe. Two clamps break, maybe. But two clamps come undone? Strange!"

On the bank of the river there were no smiles. Only the whites of their worried eyes were visible. They had failed to do what they had been commanded to do. What now?

Go back to the village after such a failure? No, that was unthinkable. The only thing left to do was try again tomorrow night. By tomorrow night the tug guiding the barges would be far downstream. If they were to be nearby when the tug tied up for the night, they must start downstream now.

With a sigh, they turned their faces downriver and began to run. Five pairs of feet picked their way along the riverbank in the moonlight and under the shady jungle trees. Over the tree roots and along the muddy bank went the five pairs of weary feet.

When morning came and the African sun shone on the wide Senegal River, the five pairs of feet were far downstream. They were very tired by now, but there was no time to rest.

By early morning they passed the swirling rapids and the undertow where number ten barge should have been pulled under the water and destroyed. Too bad they had failed last night. This was such a good place for a boat to be torn apart and all the passengers lost, maybe drowned.

Morning came. Back upriver, the family on barges seven and eight were waiting eagerly for the tiny stove to finish cooking their breakfast. Dad's huge tasty biscuits created an aroma which made it impossible to think of anything else. Chopped sausages sizzled in the skillet, waiting for the scrambled eggs to be poured into them.

After breakfast, there was nothing left to do but watch the scenery go past. They swam in the river, using the moving barge as a pier, but Dad took a lot of the fun away by requiring them to attach a line from themselves to the barge. The lines kept getting twisted as they splashed about.

By midday, they neared the rapids that came just before the narrows. The water would move swiftly through the channels, sending the barges from one bank to the other as the water sought the deepest parts of the riverbed.

All freight was fortunately attached securely or it would be flung into the river. That's what the guide book said.

Then, at the end of the rapids came the narrows. The river channel plunged between two mountains made of stone, and there was not enough bed for the river to flow in so it became very deep.

All passengers were required to be tied to the boat as securely as the freight.

They would be tied into the strong, solid "seat belts" attached to the floor with hooks. That's what the guide book said, but it was hard to imagine how it would really be. Very soon they would find out for themselves how it would be!

They could hear the rapids long before they were visible.

"I hear a train, Dad."

"No, it's a tornado."

"No, it isn't. It's the rapids!"

"Oh, the rapids!"

"I forgot about them. No, I didn't really forget, I just tried not to remember."

"I think I'm going to be scared."

"No use to be scared."

"If they would just stop the tug here, we could walk past and get back on later."

"Not me! I want to ride on them!"

"But I wish we would slow down."

"We can't. The current is pulling us so hard the tug can't hold us back."

"We're headed straight for that rock! Look out!"

Number ten barge eased around a jagged rock, seeming to miss it only by inches. It pulled number nine along with it. It dropped with much chain rattling over a short waterfall, splashing water in all directions. Number nine rocked and swayed but righted itself as number ten pulled it along.

The passengers on barges seven and eight watched in horror as number ten nosed into a whitewater pool below the falls, but at the last moment, it leveled out, pushing a wave of water over the floor of number nine. Number eight had hardly straightened up as another short waterfall appeared.

Like a jointed snake, the tugboat guided the barges down the watery stairsteps, holding them back and slowing them as much as possible. Passengers were flung this way and that against the ropes of the seat belt that held them.

No one talked. Voices could not be heard above the roar of the river. There was time to think, though, about what would have happened to one pair of barges if they had no tug to guide them through the rapids.

But it did not happen, and number nine and ten were safely attached to the string. The school teacher and his precious books was still safe.

Wangteya couldn't clear his mind. His mind jumped from the strangeness of the two clamps being undone, to the young man whose safety was his responsibility, to the teacher with the valuable books…and then back to the strangeness of it all.

It seemed that all three of these things should go to make up one problem that had the same answer, but he just couldn't think what it would be. This was his own first experience of being responsible for a family on a barge.

After another four-foot drop, the river turned sharply, and just ahead there appeared a wall of stone. The barges were headed directly into it and were certain to be crushed like a bug underfoot! Squeals and yells erupted from number eight as the rock wall bore down on them.

Then, just like a ride in an amusement park, the barges were caught in the current and pulled away from the stone mountain! White foam billowed around them, washing over the edges of the barges, amid squeals and shrieks.

Then the water of the wide river was shoved together into a narrow, deep channel, but the barges made their way through the narrow waterway like a train running on rails. The rock walls of the mountains arose high on each side, and all scenery was blocked away.

The tug fought against the speed of the narrows, and its motor was deafening as it echoed between the stone mountains on either side. For at least a quarter of a mile, they churned through the water between mountains of stone that often blocked out the sun.

Then, suddenly, the river widened and the sun shone down on them again. The water of the Senegal flowed smoothly along, just as though it had not come through the torturing rapids and narrows.

Jungle birds screamed and monkeys chattered in the overhanging trees. The water moved along as though nothing had happened!

The photographer was waiting with his camera and when the river was again in the sunshine, he began to film the clouds of birds which hovered over the water, fishing. The birds swooped and splashed into the river, always coming up with food in their beaks. They screamed and fought their aerial combat over the barges as they struggled to keep their catch from thieves, or to steal from another bird.

The feathered battle was filmed, including those mangled fish that were dropped, in the scramble, and fell back into the water, or the ones that landed with a splat on the barge boats.

"Look at all those birds!"

"Where did they all come from?" Sally wondered.

"Bird eggs," Danny answered, but no one was listening.

"Dad, why do we have so many birds here?"

"Yeah, and so many fish?"

"Hey, that's the answer. The birds are here for the fish."

"But the fish are not here for the birds."

"Why are they here?"

"That's what I asked."

"It's got to be for food. Why is there a lot of fish food here?"

"Does it grow in the rapids?"

"Maybe. What are they eating?"

"I don't know. Reach down and get one and ask him what he had for lunch."

"Ask Dad."

"He's busy with the camera now."

"I'll bet the rapids put a lot of air in the water. Remember all that foam?"

"Fish don't eat air."

"No, but they breathe it."

"Those big propellers on the tugboat would stir a lot of air into the water."

"That's what it is?"

"What, what is?"

"That's why the fish are here!"

"Because of the propellers?"

"Yes, but they didn't intend to be."

"I know. It's because of the ground-up fish, crawfish and plants that got caught in the props. The tugboat propellers make a lot of fish food every time they come through the channel and it washes down here where the water is quiet."

"Yeah, that motor has to work hard to hold the barges back from going too fast."

"Look, here comes the other tugboat around the turn!"

"Look at it go!"

"It's going to turn over...no, it isn't."

"I'm hungry. I hope the granola bars didn't get wet."

"They're still dry. Anyone else want one?"

The barges moved through the flock of feeding birds and the river became wider and wider as small streams came tumbling out of the mountains to join it. At one point, a small river added itself to them, causing the barges to bob around like corks for a short way, until the little river was absorbed into the smooth current of the Senegal.

The sunshine sunk behind the trees and Darla and Sally began to sort through the food box for something to cook.

"I'm so hungry," Darla complained. "Let's start cooking now so it will be ready quicker."

"Better not," advised her dad. "We don't know for sure if there will be anymore rough water before we stop for the night. Have another granola bar."

Through the leafy tangles of the jungle, five pairs of weary feet were still running. They traveled a bit more slowly, now, but there was no time to lose. The tugboat just passed them and would not stop for another mile or two.

They were very tired, but the job must be done and they were the ones to do it. Who knew what terrible thing would happen if they were not successful? They knew there was a chance that they would be killed if they were not successful.

The tug stopped for the night and clung close to the bank of the river. Stout chains tied it to the strong trees on the bank. The passengers were glad to take the opportunity to get off the barges and stretch their legs.

Darla and Sally quickly had water simmering for the tuna helper casserole.

"Will two boxes be enough, I wonder?"

Danny answered. "Yes, two will be enough for me, then fix what you want."

"Oh, go stuff your mouth with leaves," was Darla's gracious reply.

"I'll put on three boxes. A box is supposed to feed six people and three boxes feed eighteen. There are six of us, including Wangteya. That is three portions for each of us."

"We could make cornbread."

"No, that takes too long. We can eat crackers. I want to take a walk beside the river before it gets dark."

"I want to wade in the river and cool off."

"I'll bet Dad won't let you."

"Why?"

"Crocodiles. Look down there."

A huge lizard waddled his powerful body along on short legs and slid into the water without breaking a ripple. He arose, poking his nose out of the river, and his body looked like a floating log. Other logs just like him floated around beside him.

"Wheeewww, and I didn't even see them!"

"Still want to wade and cool off?"

"Maybe not just yet."

The photographer aimed the camera toward the river, and the crocodiles did not know they were performing in a movie. He filmed them from this side and that.

"Danny," he called, "You and Dennis bring cameras and come here."

While dinner simmered on one stove, Dad's coffee percolated on another one. Wonderful smells seemed to spread out over the water. The boys picked up cameras and ran down the river.

"Now, Danny, climb up that tree and go out on the limb. Here, put the camera strap around your head. I want you to be directly over the crocodiles when one opens his mouth."

Danny climbed up the limbs and crawled out to the end of one. The croc was directly below him.

The photographer tossed a stick into the water and the nearest croc opened his eyes. Another one moved toward him. One of the reptiles put his head over the back of the first one and opened his mouth to yawn.

Danny's camera recorded the lizard's yawn from start to finish, making a clear picture of the wavy rows of pointed teeth.

"Wait up there, Son, and see if he'll do it again."

Dennis held the third camera, steadily aimed at the lizard, and waited. He watched Danny readjust his position on the limb. Then Dennis' eyes became perfectly round in horror.

"Dad!" he whispered, hoarsely, and pointed to the brilliantly colored snake working its way up the tree.

Dad silently pushed his movie camera into Dennis' hand, and keeping his eye on the snake, he came closer to the tree. Dennis continued to watch the snake through the view-finder of the camera, cranking out shots as the snake climbed higher.

The photographer, now without a camera, had taken the small pistol from his pocket. Through the sights, he followed the progress of the snake as it reached the limb where Danny sat.

The girls had left the stove and stood silently below the tree watching the snake as it crept toward Danny. Darla picked up the camera Dennis had discarded and aimed it at her brother on the tree limb. The point of Dad's gun continued to follow the progress of the reptile.

Three feet before it reached Danny, it paused and raised its head, flicking its tongue rapidly. The crack of the piston shot echoed against the mountains and back across the river.

The vividly colored reptile clung to the limb for a moment, then slid away and began to fall toward the water. Darla snapped a shot of the brilliantly colored snake as it fell away from the limb.

The ungainly, slow moving crocodile suddenly came to life. It snapped its mouth open in a split second and caught the falling snake before it hit the water.

"Ooooh, did you see that?"

"We sure did, and so did the cameras. It's my guess that we have some very good footage there."

"Footage of what?" Danny called. "The croc wouldn't open his mouth long enough to get a shot of it."

"Did you see the snake fall?"

"What snake?"

"You didn't see the red snake?"

"No, I guess not. I was busy trying to stay on the limb and hold the camera still. Then I was trying to keep from sneezing. There's some kind of powdery dust on this limb."

"Then you'll have to wait and see it in the film. It was crawling along the limb toward you."

"It was? Then that's what Dad shot! Man, oh, man! I thought he was trying to get the crocodile to do something, and quick as it opened its mouth, I sneezed and didn't get a shot of it."

"Dad, what would have happened if you didn't have the gun?"

"I don't know, but we had it so there was no problem."

"Something's burning!"

"Oh, the supper!"

It was a good thing they had cooked three boxes of tuna helper. At least half of one box stuck to the pan and had to be scraped out on the ground.

Five pairs of weary feet belonging to five exhausted people stopped in the bushes near the tied-up tugboats, and they dropped wearily to the ground. The aroma of food made them feel even hungrier than they already were, but there was no food. Now they must wait until darkness to do the job they must do.

They waited quietly for the sun to go down, each one determining that nothing would go wrong his time. Either that, or he might not be alive to do another job.

On number eight barge, the little stove was lit for the evening hot chocolate, and for the evening devotions. Wangteya sat with them.

Dad invited, "Who will be first with a Bible verse?"

"Me first," Darla offered. "There's the verse in Psalm about the godly person being 'like the tree planted by the water, bringing forth fruit in its season.' We saw a lot of trees today but if there was any fruit, the birds got it first."

"Yes, that would be true. Sally?"

"I'm ready," agreed Sally. "Jesus said 'Lo, I am with you always, even unto the ends of the earth.' Are we at the end of the earth, or are we at the middle?"

"The earth is a ball. It doesn't have any ends," Danny objected.

"Then why did Jesus say that?" argued Sally.

"Oh, that's right," remembered Danny. "He must have been speaking figuratively, like people do when they say things like, 'the dark of the night.' Nights are always dark. I have a verse about the wind. Wise King Solomon said, 'He that makes trouble in his own family is like a person who inherits the wind.' I don't really understand it, unless it means that a family is valuable and if you lose your family because of something you did, your life would be empty like the wind."

"I imagine that's about right. Dennis, are you ready?"

"Yes. Solomon also said, 'The spider takes hold with her hands and is in kings' palaces.'"

There was a moment of silence, then, "Why did you choose that one, Dennis?"

"Because that is the only one I knew about a spider and there's one sitting on Sally's head."

"GET IT OFF!"

"Sure." Dennis flicked the spider into the air with his forefinger.

"Now mine. 'If the Lord be God, then follow Him.'" Just by looking around, we know that the Lord is God because no one else could make a world with plants and animals fitting together so well. So the next thing to do is make certain we follow Him. Now, off to sleep with you all."

The hot African sun was gone, having long ago sunk behind the mountain, and the trees beside the Senegal river became black paint brushes against a purple-gray sky. Then, as the light from the sun disappeared completely, the moon took over.

The river was a wide ribbon of sparkling ripples, reflecting gold and silver from the moon and stars. The constant chattering of the monkeys had been replaced by the occasional scream of night birds and an intermittent roar of a hunting lioness.

Five pairs of sleepy eyes forced themselves to stay awake until everyone on the tug and the barges was soundly asleep. They waited wearily, watching the boats undulate softly at the end of their clamps and safety chain. Night had settled in and it was almost time for them to get to work.

Then, one at a time, wearily, stealthily, they crept down from their hiding place in the jungle trees. They passed the pile of scorched tuna helper where Sally had scraped it. They were so hungry that even the strange smell of it seemed good, but they had no time to sample it.

Down to the edge of the water they came, as five dark shapes against a dark background. They kept their mouths shut and squenched their eyes as narrow as possible, the way a good hunter should. Moonlight shining white on teeth and eyeballs could cost a hunter his life if the enemy (be it man or beast) saw him.

The first pair of feet stepped silently into the water and waded toward the boat. The other four followed, just as soundlessly.

As they passed number nine barge, they were seen only as a group of sparkling ripples on the water. A pair of hands held to the wood of the barge for support, they were less than six feet from Dennis' foot.

One after another, the dark shapes lowered themselves into the water. Careful, urgent hands felt, first, for the safety chains. They followed the length of the chain until they reached the clasp, but the old clasp was rusted shut. In addition, a cable had been wrapped around it to secure it even more strongly.

Disappointed, they followed the length of the safety chain to number ten barge where they found the same cable protection.

Five heads eased soundlessly up from the water for breath. Then one pair of hands motioned the others to follow and all five heads were gone.

In the darkness of the water, they felt along the rusted length of the chain for the weakest link. Combining the strength of ten hands, they twisted, pouring all their strength into their grasp. Slowly, but continuously, the link separated and the end of the safety chain fell, hanging down into the muddy bottom of the river.

They arose to the surface for a breath, unmindful of bleeding hands. Then they ducked in again. There was another chain to twist apart.

They came up for air once more, allowing themselves to smile a brief signal of triumph, then four of them dived again to separate the clamps while the fifth dark shape loosened the last catch. Then they turned quickly and with silent strokes, they made for the riverbank once more.

Under the cover of bushes, they watched as the end barges drifted away from the string, moving into the current of the river, turning slowly, narrowly missing a partly submerged log. Five pairs of lungs held their breaths until the flat boat passed the log, then they breathed again as it gracefully floated downstream in the moonlight.

Asleep onboard number ten barge was a teacher with his crates of books, a native guide, and a thirteen-year-old American boy.

Five pairs of weary feet continued their journey, running along the riverbank in the direction the raft floated because their job was not yet finished.

It would have been so much easier if they had checked for safety chains last night, for, if they had, the grandson of the chief would now be a broken body, surfacing below the rapids, which they could bring safely home for a proper burial.

If that had happened, they would be heroes at the tribal camp. Then the medicine man would again be pleased.

But they had failed last night, so the job must be done the hard way. It was unfortunate that two other people would be involved, but nothing could be done about that now.

Another five miles or so down the river was the wide bend in which an unguided flat boat could run aground and stick in the sand bar. They must reach the spot before the barge, because the jolt would surely wake up the sleeping passengers. They must not be allowed to escape.

The arrows of an enemy tribe were carried on their backs for such a use as this. The body of the grandson could still be carried back to the tribe for burial, and the chief would mourn for his grandson as he had mourned for his son, and the death would be an honorable one.

If they could just succeed in this assignment, the medicine man would be happy, and village life would go on. The other bodies could be taken care of by their own people when the tugboat reached the grounded barges.

Five weary feet pushed themselves to their limit as they leaped over tree roots and dodged hanging vines. They absolutely must reach the sandbar before the barge.

Dennis Wentworth slept peacefully as the derelict barges lifted and fell with the rippling current of the river. He drifted under the over-hanging trees where birds and monkeys slept, and he passed a trio of crocodiles, sluggish from the chill of the night.

He had gone to sleep very close to a stack of crated books, because the brightness of the moonlight in his eyes had made it hard to go to sleep.

The barges dipped and rose gently as they moved along. A small jungle stream flowed into the river, creating a gentle current within the larger flow of the channel. The smaller current caught the corner of the flat boat, turning it around and drawing its companion barge with it.

The moonlight now shone directly into Dennis' face and the sudden brightness startled him instantly awake. His first thought was that he must move again, to get the moonlight out of his eyes, but he lay for a minute enjoying the coolness of the night and the gentle movements of the barge.

Strange, he thought, how the movement of the water made the barge seem to be drifting.

It was so nice to be here. So exciting, and what a lucky boy he was to have the dad he had, and to get to do such fun things. These filming trips were so nice to look forward to, during the times that Dad had to be away in the winter months.

The barges drifted gently toward the riverbank and a low limb almost touched the stacked crates of books. The moon made a pattern of tiny flashing lights as the barge moved under the limb.

MOVED UNDER THE LIMB? What in the world was going on?

Dennis sat up suddenly and looked for number eight barge where his dad would be sleeping. And where was number seven where the girls were? There was nothing around him except number nine and the moonlit water.

Of course I'm dreaming, was his first thought, but it all seemed so real. He stood up and looked at the trees moving past him. No... he was moving past the trees! He really was moving!

"Hey!" he called out above the murmur of the Senegal River. "Hey, Wangteya! Lubo! Wake up! We're drifting!"

The two men were instantly awake and standing beside Dennis, their eyes shining in the moonlight.

"Yes! Drifting!" agreed Wangteya.

"Sabotage!" announced Lubo, sadly...knowingly. "Enemies are waiting to kill me."

"Kill you? Why?" Dennis wondered.

"Tell the reasons later," commanded Wangteya. "First thing to decide what to do!"

Lubo shook his head. "Only one thing to do. Prepare defense and get ready to fight."

"Fight?"

"Yes, we fight or we die. It is clear to me now. Enemies tried to set us drifting last night. Then we would die on the rapids. They failed, so now we die from poison arrows stolen from an enemy."

"How do you know?"

"That is how my father died."

A tingle of fright bumps crawled along Dennis' arms and back. Dad and the others were sound asleep and couldn't help him. But what could they do if they had been awake? He remembered what Dad had told them over and over. When in trouble, don't waste time worrying about what you CAN'T do. That just wastes valuable time. Only think about what you CAN do.

"Where do you think the enemy is right now, Lubo?"

The teacher shrugged. "One side or the other. We will make a fort."

"Fort?"

"Did I say the wrong word? We will build a wall from the book crates. We will not be seen to be a target for arrows."

Wangteya was already heaving the crates into position. By separating them a foot apart and by stacking the smaller ones on top, they created a fortress about four feet high around number ten barge.

"Safe now if we stay on the water," Lubo decided.

"Then we'll just have to make sure we stay on the water if they come after us."

Both men shook their heads sadly. Wangteya explained, "Sandbar to stop a raft with no tug to guide it."

"How can we get past it?"

"We need what we have not."

"What?"

"A pole. Strong for shoving off from the bar before it is stuck bad."

"A pole," repeated Dennis. "Where could we get a pole? We need to be on the bank."

Lubo nodded. "But if we were on the bank, we would not need the pole. I could hide us safely. Here, on the water, we are floating geese."

"Floating geese?"

"Is that not what you say?"

"Oh, you mean sitting ducks. I see what you mean. Could we make a pole of some of these low limbs?"

"No saw for cutting through a limb strong enough."

"Okay." Danny looked around him. A pole...he had to have a pole. The barge was strong and solid and he could not pull anything loose. The crates were...."The crates! That's the answer!"

"Why the crates?"

"We need to pull off the boards to make a pole."

"Too short. No nails."

Dennis' idea was perfectly clear in his mind. "No, look...we'll pull the boards off with the nails in the ends. Then we'll pound the ends together. I wish we had a hammer."

"Hammer? Wait!" Lubo began tearing away the boards of the packing crate. He reached into a box and brought out a thick, heavy brass bookend. "This is now a hammer."

The moonlight that had seemed so bright now gave hardly enough light to see the nails they were hammering.

"Boards are thin...not strong enough to push off the sandbar."

"We'll have to put more together. Hand me some more and we'll nail them flat so it will be thick board."

The noise of the brass bookend striking against the nail heads echoed and ricocheted between the trees, but the board they were creating was now several layers thick, and very heavy.

"When we touch the sandbar," Wangteya warned, "all hands will be needed for the push."

Back on number eight barge, Danny was restless. He kept dreaming pieces of dreams that wouldn't hook themselves together. He turned over to his stomach so the moonlight would not be so bright in his face.

Nearby, Darla felt the moonlight against her closed eyelids. Was it morning already? Danny was saying something. Oh, he was just talking in his sleep. He was probably having a bad dream. She'd just wake him up so it would go away and he could get back to sleep.

"Danny?" she called, softly.

"Huh? What?"

"You are dreaming, Danny. Wake up."

"Okay." Her brother sat up and rubbed his eyes. "Darla?"

"Yeah?"

"Where's Dennis?"

"He's over...Danny! He's gone!"

"The whole barge is gone and so is the other one. DAD! WAKE UP!"

The photographer sat up. "What is it, Kitten?"

Then he saw the problem. He stood up and cupped his hands to his mouth. "HEY, MAYDAY! MAYDAY!" he called.

Then he remembered the "mayday" international distress call might not be understood on an inland tugboat. He reached into his camera case for the pistol. Its shots rang out in the night air, and lights came on all down the string of remaining barges.

"Barge overboard!" he called as he swam the short distance to shore and ran toward the tugboat. A small boat with oars was already being lowered into the water. He jumped into the boat and grabbed one set of oars.

"Barges nine and ten are loose and my son and two others are aboard them."

Two men leaped into the boat with him and together the three men bent over the oars of the small craft, slicing it through the silver water and sending ripples to either bank.

Darla, Danny, and Sally stood staring after them, speechless with fright. Last night's problem had seemed to be just a freak accident, but now it was certain to have been done on purpose. It would have been a lot of trouble for someone to go to, unless they were planning a kidnapping, or perhaps murder. MURDER! Who would want to murder Dennis?

Darla watched the empty river where her father had disappeared. A lump formed in her throat that she could not swallow. She turned to look at Sally and saw diamond tears sparkling on her cousin's cheeks, and Darla looked quickly away.

She glanced at Danny and realized he had the camera in his hand. He had filmed the speeding row boat with three sets of oars as it knifed through the ripples. It had been the only thing he could think of to do.

Downstream in number ten barge, the push pole was ready. They had done everything they could think of to do, and now there was time to become thoroughly frightened. They had no control over their speed or direction, as they drifted aimlessly, sometimes turning lazily with the current. Not fast...not slow...but steadily onward...to what?

They had plenty of time to worry.

Wangteya asked, "Will it be arrows and not guns? Do you know this?"

Lubo nodded. "If the problem is what I suspect, it will be arrows. Gun may be quicker, but gunshot in the leg, one may still live. Poison arrow in the leg...or even in the finger, one will die."

"Then we'll just have to keep from being hit, won't we?"

Five pairs of feet had at last reached their destination. The cool sand of the riverbank was comforting to the tired feet. Five exhausted bodies dropped to the sandbar for a moment of rest.

Five pairs of eyes peered anxiously upriver for the rafts to appear. It would be very soon, and they must be ready. Five arrows were prepared with poison, and held steadily, poised for use.

They must not fail this time, for there would be no other chance. If they failed again, they could consider themselves as dead men, because the blame would be upon them. No number of words would take the blame away. If they failed, they would pay. Their families would be smitten with disease, their crops would fail, and their children would be bitten by snakes.

They knew this to be true, because the medicine man had told them so. What good would be their word against that of the medicine man? Even the greatness of their chief could not protect them.

Dennis, Wangteya, and Lubo were standing inside their "fortress" made from Lubo's books, and trying to look around themselves in every direction at once. Would the attack come before the sandbar, or just as they reached it?

"If I had a spear," Lubo said, "I would feel safer."

"I wish for a spear too."

Dennis looked from one to the other. "I'd rather have a gun. Bullets go farther and faster than spears."

"Gun? Yes, gun!" Lubo exclaimed, again searching among his crates.

"Do you have a gun? Really?"

"Really! Yes! I will find it."

While Dennis and Wangteya almost held their breaths for him, Lubo searched.

"Ah! Here it is." Lubo held up a large, shiny, old fashioned six-shooter, the kind so popular in old western movies. "Gift for the Chief as souvenir of American history."

"Does it shoot?"

Lubo nodded. "They say so when I get the bullets, but I do not shoot a gun."

"Why not?" wondered Wangteya.

"I am teacher and not shooter."

"But you said you could throw a spear if you had one."

"I learned as a child. All boys of my tribe must learn. Gun shooting I did not do."

"Do you have the bullets?" Dennis asked. "I can shoot a six-shooter."

"I have bullets, yes."

Danny expertly loaded the gun by moonlight, thankful for the hours of target practice required by his dad. He grasped the loaded gun and crouched inside the fort. He felt a lot safer, now, though he had never aimed a gun at a human in his life.

Then his heart pounded and it was hard to remember to breathe, but when he held out the gun, his hand was steady. He had been very good at hitting the painted target, but now? At a human? Well, he'd just have to wait and see.

"How far are we from the sandbar?" Dennis asked.

"I cannot tell. Neither in miles or minutes, because I have been away too long, and tree limbs and riverbank makes changes. Hard to tell, also in moonlight."

Wangteya had also made the trip to the ocean, but he could not remember, either, as they were not sure how long they had been floating before waking up.

Relax, Dennis, he told himself. *Breathe normally. Be ready for whatever comes.*

Five pairs of sleep-weary eyes strained to see an approaching barge on the shining water. When the dark speck finally appeared, they were not sure that it was not a trick of the moonlight.

They watched, refusing to blink, and if the speck was just their imagination, what was making it grow larger? Surely, it was time to be ready.

They stood to their feet and positioned the arrows in their bows as they would do if they were stalking a lion or a wildebeest.

They waited with relaxed arms as they had been trained to do since they were small boys. Muscles straining before there was a need was a waste of strength. As hunters, they knew of the need to conserve their strength.

On the barge, Lubo suddenly touched Dennis' arm. "My memory is here. The sandbar is the next turn."

Dennis felt the skin prickle on his arms. Perspiration popped out on his head and his stomach began to whirl. "Hey, fellows. I think I should shoot the first shot in the air, and maybe they will run away."

Lubo answered. "Do as you think, but they will not run. They will do what they must do."

Dennis sighed. He had never thought it would be necessary to shoot at a human being. His heart began to pound harder and harder. He could hear the ka-boom, ka-boom in his ears as blood raced through his veins.

KA-BOOM, KA-BOOM! The hammering sound became louder and louder in his ears. Here he was, holding a real gun in his hand, and he was ready to aim it toward real people!

But what were they planning to do to him? *God, are you watching? Is this what I should do?*

The barges moved steadily downstream, turning in slow circles as the current pulled against the corners. A small stream entered the river near the path of the barges, causing them to undulate with the ripples. Dennis clutched the gun and checked his steadiness.

Solid as a rock. *Thank you, Dad, for the target practice that made my wrists strong.*

The barges had turned, forcing Dennis to change his position to continue to be protected by the stacks of books. Wangteya and Lubo crouched low, holding the "pole" ready to shove against the sand. Whatever happened, they were safer in the deep river than stuck against the shore.

They could see the bend of the river, and they could also see the dark shapes waiting on the sand. The attackers were so confident of the success of their plan that they made no effort to conceal themselves.

"Bad to be exposed," the teacher commented. "Means they know not to come home if they are not successful. Means they will fight to death, so be ready with gun."

The flow of the river carried the barge against the distant bank, then began to turn it, heading slowly but surely toward the wide sandbar. Around it went, one full circle, with Dennis turning to keep the dark figures in his sights, the barrel of the six-shooter resting between the piles of textbooks.

As the corner of number nine bumped against the sand, the figures on the beach, all five of them, raised their bows and ran forward.

Dennis now had them in his sights, but on sudden impulse, he pointed the six-shooter to the sky and discharged two shots.

The figures on the beach stopped, startled, and looked up.

Lugo and Wangteya used that moment to stand up from behind the crates and shove against the sandy bank with their pole. They pushed with all their strength, bracing their feet against the remaining crates of books. The barges were very heavy, but then the current caught the corner of number ten, and with help from the pole, it eased number nine from the sand. The pair of barges again began a lazy turn.

The momentarily startled figures on the beach had now recovered, and they drew their bows again. With a final shove before they ducked in to cover, the guide and the teacher succeeded in moving the barges away from the sandbar.

The volley of arrows whistled through the air, with a sound like jet-propelled mosquitoes. Two of the arrows overshot the target and splashed into the river. One arrow found its way through the crates and hit the floor of the boat.

The final two poison tips stuck fast in the crated books, ripping pages as they plunged through.

The barges were now at least twenty feet away from the bank, and still moving. One of the figures on the bank threw himself into the river to swim toward the boat. Dennis lowered the barrel of the gun to the water. Should he aim at the swimmer or save the remaining four bullets for later? Which?

While he hesitated, a rowboat from upstream barreled down on them, flooding the whole area with light from the spotlight that flashed on the rowboat. The swimmer turned back and the men on the bank disappeared into the jungle.

"DENNIS!" came the anxious call from the rowboat.

"Here, Dad," Dennis called back. "We're all okay." Sudden weariness passed over Dennis, and the old western gun slid from his hand and clattered to the floor of the barge. He stood up and looked across the water toward his father.

The errant barges had picked up speed, entering the channel current again, and the rowboat was not heavy enough to stop them. There were still very serious problems.

"We must stop," Lubo pointed out.

Wangteya agreed. "Now is time to be stuck in the sandbar."

The three people on the boat yelled at the same time. "THE POLE!"

"Hurry, before we get any deeper!"

"Here, let me help."

"Can you touch the bottom?"

"Try over here."

"I wish the pole was longer."

"Try one more time."

"No use. It's too deep."

"But it was such a good idea."

"But it didn't work."

"Wait! We can't give up yet. We may drift close to the shore again. We have to keep trying."

They pulled the pole up from the water. When they leaned over to put it on the platform, the barges began another lazy circle.

"Look," yelled Dennis. "The pole is working like a rudder!"

"Rudder?"

"To steer with."

"But is heavy. We can't hold it up very long."

The row boat was now alongside them.

"Dad, can you hand me an oar?"

"Here, Dennis. Two will be better."

Dennis handed one oar to Wangteya and they lowered the paddles into the water at one corner, bracing them against a heavy crate. The boat continued its slow turn, edging its way back toward the sandy bank.

Trees lined the shore and low limbs raked the crates of books before the boat whacked solidly against a mat of tangled tree roots.

Wangteya leaped from the boat and disappeared into the water. The barges rose and fell with the eddies and creaked noisily as the current tried to pull them back into its channel.

The strength of the current was strong and fast, but Wangteya was faster. He had quickly wrapped the trailing end of the safety chain around an exposed tree root.

The barges were now tethered solidly to the riverbank and another problem was taken care of. The photographer leaped from the row boat to the barge to see for himself that Dennis was safe.

"I'm fine, Dad, but I sure was glad to see you."

Lubo pointed out, "Sorry to say this but warriors will be back. They wait in the dark and then arrows will come flying out, and we will not know when. They will not give up what they came to do."

The photographer stroked his chin and thought. "Then we'll just have to stop them."

"Kill them with the guns?"

"Maybe not. We may be able to blind them."

The two men in the rowboat began removing the spotlight from the small boat. It was positioned on the barge facing the darkness of the jungle.

"Blinding light! Good idea! Warriors cannot get close enough to aim with light in their faces," Lubo complimented.

Wangteya asked, "Good battery to last all night?"

The photographer looked at his watch. "Not much night left," he told them. "Daylight will be in an hour or so."

"None too soon for me, Dad."

Five pairs of weary eyes stared through the jungle vines toward the spotlight until daylight, then they limped tiredly away. Failure again.

If they went back to the tribe, something terrible would happen to their families. The medicine man had told then so, and they believed him. The words of the medicine man had a strange way of coming true.

There was only one way. They would not go back to the tribe. In months or years, the old man would die, and then they could return. The chief's grandson, Lubo, would be the new chief. He had not seen their faces tonight, and he would let them come home.

Yes, that would be the best thing to do. They would have time to make up a story about why they had been gone for years.

Sadly, they stumbled away, foot-sore and hungry.

At first light of the morning, the tugboat guiding its eight remaining barges came chugging around the bend.

Using a powerful wench line, it was simple work to draw the loose barges into the line and repair the safety chain. They eased past the sandbars with no difficulty. It was so easy when they had the powerful tug to hold them back and keep them in line.

The little stove cooked biscuits as the tug led its barges on toward the ocean.

The Senegal River was wide now, and spread out across the valley. Lubo stood among his cases of books and stared at the mountains. He didn't have very much to say.

Danny stood beside him. "I'll bet you're wanting to get home again after being gone so long."

Lubo did not quickly answer.

"Aren't you?" Danny insisted.

"Please excuse the silence. I was thinking of a correct answer to your question. Yes, I will be glad to see my mother and my grandfather. I will want to see my friends, but they will not be the same as when we were boys. They will treat me differently because I am different."

"Why are you different?"

"The school. Learning made me different. We have hunger and disease in my village, but that is not strange to my people. We have always had hunger and disease. There is no reason to change that...is what the people feel. Now that I know that most of the disease and all of the hunger is not necessary, I have to tell them what I know, and they will hate me because I want them to change the way they do things."

Danny was wide-eyed with surprise. "Oh, no, Lubo. They'll all want to know how to do things better. They'll love you for what you can tell them."

Lubo smiled at Danny. "I am some years older than you, and I have learned a lot. Let me say it like this. Most people do not want to change, even if the new way is better, and if there is a reward for changing."

"Are you sure?" Danny repeated, doubtfully.

"Totally certain. Even your religious teacher, your Jesus Christ, had a very bad time when He tried to help people to have a better, easier life with a reward for changing. He tried to help His own people change, and they killed Him for his effort."

"Hmmmm, I never thought of it like that."

Lubo nodded. "But I did, and I know that if Wangteya and your brother had not been on my barge, I too would be dead, and all the teaching books would become food for the snails in the river."

"But, Lubo, that didn't happen. My dad tells us kids not to waste time worrying about something that could have gone wrong, but didn't."

Lubo nodded again. "And he is right, but it was in my mind to think of words to thank all of you for being a friend these two days. I will be very lonely and I will badly need good friends for the next few years, if I get to do what I want to do. I will be glad of my memories of your family while I am alone."

"Oh, you don't have to thank us. Look, Lubo! I see a lot of people on the riverbank way down there. Look!"

"I know, Danny, and I did not look because my eyes will cry when I do. The crowd of people are from my village, come down to welcome me home."

"Well, see there? They love you. It won't be so bad."

"Danny?"

"Yes, Lubo?"

"Not everyone is waiting on the bank. My enemies are waiting back in the village. They will wait for the right time, and they will try again to kill me. That is one thing I know."

"Oh."

"But enough of that. I want to ask you for a favor, young Danny."

"Anything you want!"

"I want you to come to my village sometime...you and your brother. Wait a year or two years to give me time to make changes and bring education, then you must come with your family and your cameras, and make pictures of the good things that will happen in my village. Will you promise?"

"Yes, Lubo. I will promise to try very hard. It might be later than two years, but if I cannot come with my family, I promise I'll try to come alone."

Lubo smiled, "But be sure to bring the brave brother who got sick at the thought of shooting the gun at a person."

"Dennis got sick? Really?"

"Very sick, but it must be our secret. He tried so hard to be brave, and he was successful. Being sick does not make one less brave, when he has to face doing something hard to do."

His brother could only consider the matter in silence. *Hmmmm.*

Back on number eight barge, the photographer was filming the flock of birds that had swooped and darted over the river, and then returned to the high stone-faced cliffs.

"Look, Dad! There are a lot of fish here and the birds just fly around up there."

"Are they scared of us?"

"Are they just learning to fly?"

"No, that wouldn't be right, because there are too many of them."

"They fly too fast to be babies."

"Dad?"

"What, Kitten?"

"What kind of birds are those?"

"Those are called 'bee-eaters.'"

"Bee-eaters?"

"Yes, because they eat insects on the wing and a large number of the insects here are bees. We just don't see them."

"Oh, that's like the 'millet eaters' we saw in east Africa that steal crops from the native farmers. What was that African name?"

"Quealea? Yes, but even the quealea birds also catch insects when they have babies to feed, so perhaps they do not harm the farmers as much as the farmers think they do. Perhaps the birds pay for the grain they steal by removing harmful insects that would steal even more grain than they do."

"They don't feed the baby birds the seeds like they eat?"

"No, at least they'd rather not. Most seed-eating birds like to have worms for their nestlings. Mashed grasshoppers are also a favorite food for chicks. Perhaps the seeds are harder for the babies to digest than insects."

"Shhhooeeee! I believe I'd rather have seeds than smashed bugs. Look at the people, Dad! That must be Lubo's village."

The noisy crowd of people were waiting on the bank. It sounded like a party, and they were dressed in brilliantly beautiful colors and were singing happy songs.

Closest to the river stood an old man wearing a red and purple robe, smiling, watching the tugboat approach. He watched as the boat was tied securely to a tree and the rowboat was lowered.

Lubo stepped into the rowboat, trying not to look toward his grandfather. It was not fitting that a man, almost grown as he was, and soon to be the next chief, should be seen with signs of crying on his face.

Yet, he could feel the tears now gathering in pools behind his black eyes.

The oarsmen pulled the boat toward the brilliantly dressed old man, who held out his arms. In spite of his efforts, Lubo was sobbing as he ran to his grandfather.

Darla and Sally sat on the edge of number eight barge and watched. Darla sniffed and swallowed twice.

Sally wiped her cheek.

"Darla?"

"What?"

"How would you feel if you hadn't seen your family for six years?"

"Probably just the way Lubo feels."

The waiting people crowded around Lubo and his grandfather, reaching out their hands to touch their returning tribe member on the arm or head, or even on his clothing.

"They sure are glad to see him come home. Everyone in the whole town must love him," observed Sally.

Danny opened his mouth to say something but closed it again. Talking about it here would not help Lubo with what he had to do, and if the girls wanted to think he was loved by everyone, that was all right.

They wouldn't like the truth if they heard it, so he would just keep still. Some feelings were hard to explain.

The crates of books were opened and armloads of them were distributed into the arms of adults and children who were eager to carry them into the village.

Lubo, walking beside the grandfather, turned to wave as the tugboat chugged away down the river.

After the experience of the run-away barge, the rest of the trip seemed very calm.

There was time to take a nap in the mosquito net tent, rocked by the gentle motion of the water.

There was time to sit on the edge of the barge and dangle feet in the water, watching their father as he clicked the camera toward dozens of scenes.

The last to be filmed were the seagulls, flying in from the ocean to pluck fish from the water of the mouth of the Senegal River. One gull had speared a fish that was too heavy, and though he flapped furiously, he could not climb into the sky.

Another gull would like to steal the fish, and also speared it with his bill. The first bird refused to let go, and together the two birds flew, their wings beating furiously together, holding to the same fish. The good part of it was, together they had strength enough to get the huge fish into the air.

Who could know what would happen when they both tried to eat it? Wouldn't that be a good final shot…if they just had it?

Then the photographer and his family were back in the jet that they had left at the mouth of the river. The tiny stoves were covered with the dust of Africa, but that could be cleaned later.

The mosquito nets had been snagged in many places, and it would take a lot of thread and time to repair them.

Cameras and other equipment were packed carefully and loaded onto the jet. A few granola bars waited to be snacked on, if someone got hungry. Really, really hungry.

But most of all, eyes drooped with weariness from all the sights of the past week, and minds were so full of experiences, it was impossible to remember every single one. All of that would come later when the film shots were put together, cut apart and reattached in good order.

Danny would get to see the red snake climbing into his tree, and Dad would see the dark shape of himself in the rowboat, knifing through the water. The next days would be bursting with memories. Some to be enjoyed now and others to be enjoyed later...a lot later.

Only the pilot was awake when the jet received clearance to take off.

"Beechking ICU2 to Tower...."

Then they were back in Miami, Florida, spending the night in the tiny jet.

"We can't have hot chocolate," complained Darla.

"Because we can't operate the stove in an enclosure."

"I know that. I just wanted hot chocolate. It's easier to think of my Bible verse for devotion if I can sniff the steam of a cup of hot chocolate."

"I thought of one, Dad."

"All right, Dennis."

"I looked it up, and it is in Proverbs 4:18. 'The path of the just is as the shining light, that shineth more and more.' Just when I was sure I would be shot with a poison arrow, here you came with the spotlight that chased the enemy away. The next thing I worried about was whether the batteries were strong, but they lasted all the rest of the night. I think that may be the best verse I ever thought of."

"Very good. Next? Danny?"

"Mine is something Lubo knew. The verse says that 'a prophet is not always accepted by his own people,' but I think it might be the same for a teacher. He thinks the next few years may be hard and dangerous, and he will not be successful until the young children he teaches can grow up."

"Also very good. Darla?"

"I keep thinking of the creation. 'Darkness was on the face of the earth.' Then God made the sun and moon to give light. If the moonlight had not woke Dennis up, he would not have been ready to fight. If it had not made me wake up, I would not have heard Danny talking in his sleep. And he wouldn't have been talking in his sleep if he had not turned over on his stomach to keep the moonlight out of his eyes. See how it all works out?"

"Yes, it all works out. Sally?"

"I keep thinking about how scared I was when we knew Dennis was gone, and I thought about David saying, 'I will fear no evil, for thou art with me.' The trouble is, I did fear, and didn't think about trusting God until later. I'm sorry about that."

The photographer nodded his understanding. "God knows we forget sometimes, Sally. Mine is, 'The eyes of the Lord are in every place, beholding the evil and the good.' When we think about it, that just about covers everything. So crawl into your sleeping bags and get to sleep."

"Dad?"

"What, Kitten?"

"I wanted to think of a verse about being very, very crowded and hardly having room to sleep, but I couldn't. There really isn't one that says that, is there?"

"Well, hang in there, and we'll be home. There's lots of room in Missouri."

It was some days later when they gathered around the TV, waiting for their documentary to come on.

So many animals used the water of the Senegal River. Birds, fish, insects, large furry mammals, lizards, and snakes (the little red snake showed brightly against the gray of the tree trunk as it climbed by hooking its scales onto the rough bark of the tree, easing out on the limb, and falling into the open mouth of the crocodile).

Interspersed among the scenes were shots of the loaded barge. For, after all, The barge used the water to float on.

Finally came the scene of the two gulls with their beaks speared into the same large fish, flapped their wings furiously, climbing into the blue African sky.

Sitting here on the soft carpet of their Missouri home, eating popcorn and chips, Africa seemed a lifetime away.

"Can we go back to Africa, Dad?"

"Probably, but you will go to bed first."

"Aw, Dad...."

THE CASE OF THE STOLEN SISTER

T he shiny little jet airplane taxied to the end of the runway and waited for permission to take off. The control tower was busy assigning airspace as one after another of the waiting aircraft moved into position.

Finally the cockpit radio crackled with static, then announced loudly, "Tower to Beechking ICU2, cleared for takeoff on runway 12. Have a good flight."

The pilot of the jet picked up his microphone. "Beechking ICU2 to Springfield Tower. Acknowledged."

The thirteen-year-old triplets, Darla, Danny and Dennis Wentworth, seat belts fastened, felt the airplane begin to move. Photographer Montgomery Wentworth, their father, sat at the controls. At the end of the runway, the plane nosed into the air and climbed steadily to the sky. The town of Springfield, Missouri, became a toy village below them and then it disappeared into the green of the trees and mountains.

The small jet circled into its flight path heading south. Below it was Table Rock Lake, a shiny blue rug reflecting the pale blue of the sky and the sparkling shimmer as it mirrored the morning sun. The river flowing into it was a silver ribbon, winding around the mountain and falling in foamy cascades over the precipices caused by the rock bluffs.

The mountains of southern Missouri and of northern Arkansas were threaded with gray lines of highway and dotted with fields of green crops and many small lakes of deep blue. Farms with their tiny ponds were sprinkled about on the sides of the hills.

The Beechking passed over the twin basins of Lake Fort Smith near the tiny Arkansas town of Mountainburg, then it was over the towns of Alma, Van Buren, and then the larger city of Fort Smith, practically encircled by the lazy Arkansas River.

Then came Oklahoma. The mountains flattened into treeless spots of red dirt and the square blocks of green wheat fields. The jet crossed the Red River into Texas.

The waters of the gulf were beautiful on a sunshiny day. The blue of the sky was reflected back as many shades of blue with turquoise overtones, patterned with whitecaps off the tips of the waves. Even when the weather was stormy, the ocean was beautiful. The storms turned the blues to indigo purple and black, and its strong winds upset the waves and brought up the tangle of greenish seaweeds. The water was always beautiful, but today was not stormy so it shimmered peacefully.

The Control Tower at Monterrey was informed of their presence and the voice on the radio wished them a pleasant journey. Darla was on page 125 of her library book, and her brothers were tied at 17 checker games each. One more game to break the tie, they decided, then that would be enough checkers for one day. They were already seeing red and black spots before their eyes.

Darla put a marker in her book and went forward to sit beside her father.

"Hello, Kitten," he greeted her.

"Hi, Dad."

They flew over a few more miles of red and brown landscape.

"Are you getting bored?" Darla's father asked her.

"No, just lonely. I don't see why Sally couldn't come along."

"I do," he answered her, surprisingly.

"You do? Why?"

"Your cousin has parents who love her and think she should spend some time with them. If your mother was still alive, she would no doubt be wanting you to stay with her occasionally instead of shooting off into the sky with me all the time."

"But, Dad, don't you think Mom would have wanted to come with us?"

"Sometimes, perhaps, but she would want to stay home sometimes, too."

"Oh. But it really isn't fair."

"What isn't fair?"

"It isn't fair that Dennis and Danny have each other and I have no one when Sally doesn't come along."

"I can understand that. I don't have anyone, either. Perhaps we'll just have to stick together on this trip. Just you and me."

Darla grinned at her father. "Do you really think you can stand me that long?"

"I don't know, Kitten, but we can try it and see."

"Dad, about those carvings we are going to be filming, how many are there?"

"Oh, hundreds, at least. They are scattered all over Mexico and Guatemala. We will never count them accurately because we can never find them all."

"Oh. But if the Mexican Government wants to catalog a complete set of ancient Indian wood carvings and totem poles, why don't they just order them all to be brought to the historical museum in Mexico City? Then everyone could come and see them."

"That sounds like a good idea, Kitten, and I'm sure they would do that if they could, but they can't. Many of the carvings are privately owned and no amount of money would buy them, and some other of the carvings belong to the Guatemalan government, and those are not for sale. Then, too, some of the carvings were made into living trees, and even though the trees are now dead, they are still attached to the ground and are preserved. These could not be moved without damage. They decided the best they could hope for was a fairly complete set of very good pictures for their ancient history and cultural exhibit."

"Oh, Dad, weren't you going to make extra pictures for your friend, Tony, over at the library?"

"Yes, but not for him, exactly. The extra pictures will be for the library in return for partial financing of this trip. They pay money, they get pictures. With the Mexican Government, the library and

Public Broadcasting System in Kansas all cooperating, the pictures will be cheaper for all of them. It is also possible that other museums will be interested in them."

"You mean we will get a lot of money for these pictures?"

"Enough." Her dad nodded.

A lot of miles passed under them and the little plane left the shoreline of the Gulf of Mexico to proceed inland.

"I'm hungry," complained Darla.

"Really? Did we run out of granola bars?"

"Aw, Dad, that's not what I want. I'm sure we have at least two cases of the bars. The boys must have thought we would be gone for a month. They loaded them on. Guess what I really want."

"Spaghetti?" guessed her dad with a grin.

"Oh, of course not! I want tacos and sopapillas with honey."

"But do you think we can find them in Mexico City?"

"Aw, Dad, tacos are Mexican food and we are in Mexico. How could we keep from finding them here somewhere?"

"Oh, so you think the Taco Shack has a restaurant here, just like back home?"

"Aw, Daddy!"

It was very quiet inside the airplane except for the soft sound of music coming from the CD player. There was no sound at all coming from the checker players.

"Did we loose the boys somewhere back there? I haven't heard a sound for miles."

Darla turned to look back at her brothers. "They're asleep, Dad. Both of them. The last game of checkers is still on the board. They must have gone to sleep at the exact same instant because this game was to be a tie-breaker."

"Watch me wake them up. Are they in their seat belts?"

"Yes, they are. Is that Mexico City down there?"

"It sure is. Here we go." He picked up the mike. "Beechking ICU2 to Mexico City Tower...."

The gentle touch down of the wheels jarred the checkerboard just a little, causing each checker to slide cornerways for about one and one half blocks. The outside row of checkers fell into Dennis' lap.

"Huh?" he said, startling awake.

Danny yawned. "My turn?"

"I don't remember. Look, the checkers all slid off. But I was ahead, remember?"

"No, you weren't. I remember making a king and then it was your turn."

"Yeah, and I was ahead."

"But I had more kings and I would have won."

"That doesn't count. I had more checkers and I would have made them kings."

"That doesn't count, either."

"Does, too."

Darla turned toward her father. "I think they're awake, Dad."

"Does not."

"Does, too."

"Does not."

"That's enough, boys. It's chow time and we're looking for a place to get tacos before we check into the hotel."

"I want seven."

"I want a burrito, too."

"Can we have sour cream on them?"

"Eat anything you want but I don't you up sick all night. Promise?"

"But Dad, we were only sick when we had that contest to see how many chips and olives we could eat."

"You heard me, boys."

The man wearing the expensive suit and silk shirt was talking with Gilberto and Juan. "Like I told you in the advertisement, I need two very strong men who can also be very sneaky. Tell me about yourselves."

Gilberto pushed up his sleeve and rippled the muscles of his upper arm. "Muscle, see? From loading cargo for a long day."

The man in the silk shirt seemed properly impressed. "But can you be sneaky?"

"Why? To catch a cat? Or a tiger? Or will we slip up on a bird or a snake? What is there to be sneaky for? We can be sneaky and strong."

The man nodded. These men seemed capable and he wanted to get this business over. Interviewing applicants was not something he enjoyed. "I want someone to sneak up on a little girl."

"A nina? Is easy!"

"Oh, it might not be so easy."

Juan nodded agreement with his friend. "Is easy. A little girl would be like candy to be handled. She take candy, we take her. We pick her up and run. Is easy."

But the other man shook his head. "This girl is not so little. She's twelve or thirteen years old and she will know not to take candy from strangers. You'll have to pick a good time when she's alone, and I'm sure it will take both of you to hold her."

"All right if she screams? Girl thirteen years old, she could have high voice."

Juan nodded, putting his fingers in his ears and cringing as though he could hear the shrill sound of her scream.

"Oh, no. She mustn't yell."

"You want hand on the mouth?" Gilberto shook his head quickly. "No hand on the mouth. Girls bite."

Then the man in the silk shirt took an adhesive plaster from his brief case. "Here's what you do," he explained. "You must peel off the back and slap this over her mouth, then grab her hands so she can't peel it off. And be sure you don't slap it over her nose. We don't want her dead from suffocation."

Gilberto and Juan examined the plaster. Juan looked at the man, squinting his eyes in puzzlement. "Why you want this girl? For what you do with her?"

The other man smiled pleasantly. "I'm glad you asked. That little girl was kidnapped from her parents in California and they have asked me to bring her back to them."

"Then why not hand to the girl a message saying to run to you and you help get her back? We could do that for you. We could take you to her."

"No, we can't do that. If we follow them around looking for a chance to get a message to them, they will get suspicious. But you, this is your country and no one will notice if you follow them.

Besides, this is how I want it done and I am the one who is paying for it. Now do you want the job or do I keep looking for someone else?"

"No, no. We help."

Juan nodded. "We help. No more talking."

"All right. Now there is a man with her, and his twin boys will be along. They are about the same age as the girl. The four of them are at the hotel right now, eating dinner. They are checked into a room on the second floor, room 204. You just go over there and stay out of sight until you get her."

"But the man, he would watch a little girl, and maybe shoot."

"No. He won't shoot you with a gun. He won't even have a gun with him because he is a photographer and he only shoots pictures. And the boys, they are very nosey and they will be looking around a lot, and they may even go off by themselves. That would give you a chance to get close. You see why I wanted to be sure you were strong. But let me tell you one thing."

"What?"

"If you get yourselves caught by that man or by the police, you never heard of me. We have never met and I'll tell the police I never saw you in my whole life. Do you understand?"

"We understand."

"We never get caught, so there is no problem."

The men nodded. "We catch little girl for her mama."

"Huh?"

"For her mama," Gilberto repeated. "We catch the little girl for you to take to her California mama. You say?"

"Oh, yes. For her mama. Her California mama is very anxious to get her back."

Gilberto and Juan left, walking toward the hotel and discussing how they would spend the American dollars they would get for helping the little girl back to her mama. This was the way a job should be, helping people and getting paid. So much better than loading trucks at the dock all day in the heat.

At a safe distance, they followed the Wentworths up to their room and stationed themselves outside to watch the door all night. They decided they would take turns sleeping, and in a very short time the lights went out in Room 204.

The Wentworths were up early and together they went down to breakfast. Juan and Gilberto were watching but they had absolutely no chance to get the little girl. She stayed very close to the man and the boys, and if they did not know better, they would have thought she belonged there. But, of course, all Americans looked alike so it was just their imagination that she looked like the boys. She seemed to be having fun and didn't even seem as though she missed her California mama, but who could tell about Americans?

After the family ate, a car came and took them away and the two men had no way to follow. They called the man in the silk shirt.

"Don't tell me your problems," he yelled at them angrily. "Either you can do the job or you can't. If you can't do it, I'll get someone else. If they didn't take their luggage with them, they'll be back. You will just have to wait there for them."

Juan and Gilberto had no other choice but to do just that, so they sighed and settled down to wait. Gilberto's rattly old car was parked close to the hotel entrance so they could observe the doorway, but they were forced to move around a bit to avoid attracting attention.

The car from the hotel took the Wentworths to the Airpark where the helicopter was waiting to take them away for their day's filming.

"Not as big as ours, huh, Dad?" observed Danny as he inspected the aircraft.

"No, son, but it will be big enough. We won't be taking all of that camping gear we usually carry because we will be back at the hotel for the night."

In minutes, they were in the helicopter lifting off to photograph the native woodcarvings of Mexico. These had been located in advance and arrangements with the owners had been made, so they would be expected.

"Darla, hand me the map, please." Danny asked above the sound of the chopper engine.

The boys spread the paper out between them.

"There is the first stop," Danny pointed out as he touched the red cross mark with his finger. "Dad, there isn't even a tiny town close to the "X" mark."

"Dad, what's there?" Darla asked.

Dennis butted in, "A red "X", that's what's there."

Darla ignored him. "What is that little number beside the "X"?"

Danny leaned down to the map. "Let's see. It's a three."

"All right, I've got it. It says so, right here. Three, that must be the wooden carving of the Indian girl with the jewel eyes. Would the girl be Indian or Spanish?"

"We'll have to see, won't we?"

Then Mr. Wentworth's voice sounded above the motor. "Danny, reach in the satchel there beside you and get out the small recorder. There are fresh batteries there beside it. I want you to go ahead and put them in the machine."

"But, Dad, aren't we just taking still pictures, not moving pictures? Why would we need sound?"

"Yes, Danny, we are taking still pictures, but sometimes we hear stories and legends and old folk tales that make the pictures more interesting. We'll also be taking some movie film for our own use."

Danny fitted the batteries into the small cassette recorder. "Who's going to have to carry the cassette, Dad? I want a camera."

"Don't worry about that, Danny. There are enough of us to do the job. You may carry a still camera and Darla will take the recorder. Dennis, you will carry the movie camera and be ready if anything interesting happens. Darla, you will have to be ready to start a conversation and always be where the talking is going on. Things like local stories make our film a lot more valuable.

"Sure Dad."

Darla thought, *why not?* It might be fun to snoop around with a microphone in her pocket, listening and talking, pretending to be a reporter. Actually, come to think about it, why would the ancient people make these wooden images that were so valued? That was a good question. The carving must have taken a long time to make. Weren't they busy raising corn and beans? Who could eat a carving after it was done, and it took a lot of time to do them. The carvings must have been very important to them.

They arrived at the red "X" mark. A young Mexican man met them and ushered them into the large adobe house where a young woman smiled and urged them onward toward the object of art.

There, on the wall, was the wood carving. The smooth wooden face of the figure looked almost like marble...cool and life like. A beautiful face, it was, of an Indian (Spanish?) girl and she smiled at them from the wall. The lips of the wooden lady were parted, slightly turned up at the corners, and the skin appeared to be of soft, tan velvet rather than hard wood.

The lady's nose was smooth and straight, and each nostril was delicately formed. Flowing hair was brought around the head and neck to fan out across one shoulder. The waves of the hair appeared to have just that instant been combed, and the delicate coils of the curls were shaped to stay in place for centuries. In fact, the carving was already over one hundred years old.

But, for all the beauty of the face, the most spectacular thing about it was the eyes. They had been shaped with the same skill as the rest of the creation, but where the pupils of the eyes would be, two shining sapphires glowed. Also, wherever a person stood in the room, the girl in the carving appeared to be looking directly at them. The brilliant eyes and the small smile on her lips made her seem to be listening with interest to what was being said to her.

How did they do it? She seemed to be almost alive.

"Look, Dad, when I stand here she watches me and when I go over there, she still looks at me. I want to get all sides of the picture to show how she seems to see everything. She looks every way at once, Dad!"

"She does, at that," agreed his father, as Danny moved here and there searching for the best angles.

The owners of the carving stood by and smiled, please that their wall decoration was considered important and they were happy that their talented, long-ago ancestor was so honored. They waited, leaning against the wall, anxious to allow the photographer as many pictures as he wanted.

Darla stepped toward the young woman and in her very best Spanish asked, "Who make the carving? My name is Darla."

"Darla? I am Marita. Who made it? The carving was special gift for the grandmother of my mother by her husband."

"But who made it?" insisted Darla.

"Who? The husband, of course, made it. He married a very young bride and he took her away from her family. She cry all the time from being lonesome for her family. Her mama and papa she miss very much but the most thing she miss is her sister to talk to. Her husband loves her and sees her tears so he wants to make a sister for her to talk to and think about. He sees her cry and cry, so he takes the wood and carves it away so his wife's sister's face can come out."

"Really?"

"They say it happened really."

"But, Marita, there is one thing I don't understand."

"Ask me."

"The eyes. If he wanted a picture to look exactly like the sister of his bride, why would he make the eyes that way?"

"The eyes? Why?"

"But...shouldn't they be brown?"

"Like me? Oh, no. She had eyes blue like the stone and my mother's grandmother have blue eyes. My grandmother have blue eyes, but my mother, her eyes were like mine. Brown."

"Really?" exclaimed Darla. "They were really supposed to be blue? That is such a beautiful story. I can see why you would want to keep the carving and never let any one have it."

"But I will."

"You will let someone have it? The museum?"

Marita shook her head. "Ah, no. It will never belong to anyone but my little girl. My nina named Rosita."

"You have a little girl?"

"Oh, my Rosita. You want to see her, yes?"

"May I?"

"She sleep. I wake her up."

"Oh, no. Let her take her nap. I'll look at her while she sleeps."

"Rosita may sleep anytime. Now she will wake up for you to see."

"But, surely...."

"Come," Marita instructed as she left the room. Darla followed. Rosita was not asleep but was sitting on her bed, fully awake. She was a tiny waif of a girl, perhaps three or three and a half years old.

"Ah? The Rosita is awake? Come to Mama."

The little girl flashed a quick smile and slid off the bed. She padded across the cool stone floor on bare feet and held her arms up to her mama. Marita picked her up.

"Look, Rosita, the senorita has come to see us. Look at her."

Little Rosita turned toward Darla and smiled. Darla caught her breath as she saw the little girl's eyes. They were a bright, brilliant blue, and they glowed with deep color just the same as the sapphires in the carving.

"Her eyes?" exclaimed Darla.

"Oh, yes! Eyes of her mama's ancestor. Blue like the stone." Marita smiled with pride as she hugged her small daughter.

The wide blue eyes of the little girl stared at Darla for a moment, then she wriggled to get down and she dashed away. Darla and Marita watched her leave the room and it was then that Darla noticed the furniture of the room. The little girl's bed and chest were carved with complete pictures of flowers growing and small animals playing among the plants.

"How beautiful?" Darla complimented. "Who carved this? Did your mother's grandfather do this, too?"

The young woman shook her head.

"Then who?" insisted Darla.

"I cannot say."

"You don't know?"

"I know."

"Then who? Please tell me."

"Nobody."

"Nobody? But somebody did it."

Marita ducked her head. "I am nobody."

"You? Did you do the carving? Really, did you do it? May I take a picture of it, please? Did you really do it?"

"I am ashamed to waste the time, and I cannot say."

"You did do it! But how? It looks so very difficult to do."

"Please, no," the young Mexican woman insisted. "It is I who would waste time with the knife and hammer and would waste the sandstone to make the pictures for my little girl...."

"Do let us take pictures of it? May I?"

"Oh, no. I would be ashamed."

"But the pictures you carved are as pretty as the girl in the other room. Please show me how you do it?"

"Ah, is nothing. I do nothing but move away the wood that does not belong in the picture. Take knife, so, and hammer in the hand...like so, and tap-tap-tap. The knife blade scoops up little bits of wood to move them out of the way. See? Move the knife here and tap-tap lets the flower bloom. Cut away more wood and the little bird will sing in the sky." Marita smiled at Darla. "The bird wanted to be free and it waited in the wood, calling me to set it free." Then she ducked her head. "Please do not listen to the silly story of my wasted time."

Darla shook her head. Marita must not stop talking. She must continue her story, so Darla must ask more questions. "How do you make it so smooth? Tell me how you do it?"

"Ah, yes. The smooth part. The round stone made of sand takes off the rough places. Tiny hard rocks inside the big rock bite off tiny pieces of wood and dust, then the petal of the flower is smooth. It is a balance. Hard stone makes soft flowers. See the hard tree trunks? Soft brush of reeds makes hard tree bark. Is more balance. Hard makes soft and soft makes hard."

Darla reached out a finger to touch the wing of the bird decorating the foot panel of the girl's bed. "But the bird, how do you get the feathers to look so real?"

The young woman's brown eyes shone. "Ah, the bird. It would have to have the feathers to fly. If it would not fly, it would not be right to let it come out of the wood. So it needs feathers. See the knife and the hammer? Put lightly this way and that way and tap-tap with the lightness of a feather, and the feather is there. Feathers for the wing and for the tail. Feathers were always there and I just let them come out. I did it for the bird."

"Then what do you do? After the sand stone, I mean."

"After? Just the oil."

"Oil?"

"Brush the oil with the tiny hair brush, made with hair of a kitten. Soft, like a whisper, the oil is fed to the wood. The wood drinks up the olive oil and more oil and more oil. Then is the time to shine. The sheep wool makes the shine."

"Sheep wool? Do you grow sheep?"

"Ah, yes. Wool for making rugs and bed covers. Maybe clothes."

"And the sheep wool makes the wood shine?"

The Mexican woman nodded. "Wool makes the shine."

Dennis had entered the room just after Rosita had run out the door and he had been filming the carved furniture and the actions of the carver while she talked with Darla. Danny and his dad stood in the door and watched.

The story of the carved furniture was obviously over and Darla complimented, "It's so very beautiful! I think it may even be prettier than the face of the girl in the other room."

The brown eyes popped open, wide and round. "Oh, no! This is only waste of time of one whose hands should be grinding corn. Not like the hands of my mother's grandfather. Please do not say!"

"Oh, but it is," insisted Darla.

Marita's husband came and stood by her, smiling. "Very good, I say to her and she still say it is nothing. I say she gets her hands from her ancestor to do the carving, and she say hush or bad luck will come. But it is permitted that I say I am proud she is my wife and I say she does not waste time. Ground corn is eaten today and forgotten tomorrow, but the pictures in the wood will bring happiness to our Rosita for all her life."

Marita bowed her head, but Dennis' camera picked up the small smile of pleasure at her husband's words.

The young man picked up a small stool from beside the bed. "See the plants and flowers, but look again at the butterfly on the flowers. See another butterfly come flying through the sky. But look down and see tiny worm on the stem? It is a hungry worm and has eaten into the leaf. See?"

Darla examined the carving more closely. "Oh, I see it! How did you make those tiny, tiny worm holes?"

Marita smiled. "Hard, sharp sand and a tap-tap-tap. Sand grains eat holes like the worm, when the hammer taps."

"Hmmmm," commented Darla. "I would never have thought of that, but of course, I am not a woodcarver."

Marita nodded. "Not me either, but my mama's grandfather, he was a carver and what he makes is beautiful for many years. The picture he made will belong to my Rosita after me."

The story was finished. Marita moved toward the doorway and everyone left the tiny bedroom, and the scene that was more interesting than the one in the other room, that they had spent so much effort to find and time to film. Together these stories made a very profitable morning.

They left the adobe house and went to another location where an ancient log building was decorated with the carvings of an unknown artist, probably centuries ago. From there they went to the home of the owners of a room-divider panel, carved into a lattice, completely covered with vines and ripening grapes.

The lattice of the room divider had diamond shaped openings in the lattice work, and was so skillfully carved that whichever side of it you stood, it was still a beautiful work of art. The carved leaves lay delicately against the wood and each grape was smoothly rounded. It was a valued heirloom to its owners, and it was almost as beautiful as Rosita's bedroom furniture.

By now the sun was going down and it was near dinner time. Stomachs were empty and rumbling and the tantalizing smell of the food being prepared made it difficult to think of other things.

"Stay and eat with us," came the friendly invitation, and Dennis was already looking for a place to sit down when his father declined, thanking the family kindly.

"But, Dad...?"

"Into the helicopter, Son."

The little white-haired Mexican lady looked at him in sympathy. She gathered up a handful of ripe avocados and held them out to Dennis. "Three...for you and the others to keep you from starving," she explained.

Dennis looked quickly toward his father who nodded approval. "Thanks," he was quick to say. "I love avocados."

The little lady smiled. "Avocadoes are good for growing strong."

The helicopter swung up and over the trees and mountains back to Mexico City. "I think I've had all the granola bars I want for a while, Dad. Fly faster, so we can get some food, please."

"That food back there looked really good."

"And they would have let us eat with them."

"But Dad wouldn't let us."

"And the food was all fixed and ready."

"And they had a lot of it."

"The peppers smelled really hot."

"You can't smell hot, silly."

"Then how come they made my nose burn?"

"I wanted that tostado."

"Yeah, but all you got was an avocado."

"Yeah, that's all we all got."

"Avocados don't go so good with granola bars."

"Right, but I'd eat another one if I had it."

Mr. Wentworth guided the helicopter along its invisible path through the sky. "If you three are trying to make me feel guilty, you're wasting your time and strength. I'd rather have you hungry than sick. Eating different food is a good way to get a belly ache and I don't want any sick kids. And if you're that weak from hunger, perhaps you should keep still and save your strength. Or you can have another granola bar."

"Yuk!"

"Aw...Dad...."

"Hey, look! I see the lights of Mexico City ahead. That is Mexico City, isn't it?"

"It has to be. That's right where we left it."

"Unless they moved it while we were gone."

"I'll take it, whatever it is."

At the Airpark in Mexico City, they called for a car to take them back to the hotel. As they walked into the door, Gilberto nudged Juan and pointed.

"They're back."

From the evening darkness of the old car, Juan nodded agreement. "They've still got the little girl, too."

"Did you think they would dump her somewhere? They are thinking how much money they will get out of her, I'd bet," commented Gilberto, as he got out of the car.

"Then why haven't they sent a note for the ransom money? They ain't acting like no kidnappers I ever heard about," Juan objected.

"And how many you ever heard about? You think you are some kind of expert? Come on before we lose them, again."

Juan and Gilberto followed the Wentworths into the restaurant. The girl sat down between the man and the boys. She followed the man closely as they went up the stairs to their room. There was no chance to grab her then, so they settled down in the hall outside the door to wait.

Gilberto complained, "We need to put us a bell on that door so we can both sleep."

But Juan answered, "Hush up and let me sleep, its my turn now. We can talk on your own sleeping time if you want to."

Inside room 204, the photographer cleaned his camera lens and put away the cameras and the recorder.

"Time for evening devotion," he announced. "Let's have our Bible verses before someone goes off to sleep. Pick out a good verse that you remember and tell us why you thought of that particular one."

"I'm ready," Dennis announced. "Mine is 'Whatsoever your hands find to do, do it with all your might.' Those woodcarvers used their hands and strength. That must have been one of the things God was talking about."

"I'm sure of it. Now Danny?"

"I wish I had my Bible, Dad because I wanted a verse about hands doing things. Dennis got the only one I remember, but I know there must be another one but I can't remember. So I'll have to take this one. 'Love one another.' All of the things we looked at today were made by someone for someone else that they loved."

"Good. Darla?"

"I'm ready. I know I have used this one before but this time it fits better than at any other time. 'The eyes of the Lord are in every place, beholding the evil and the good.' Now I have a good idea of how God's eyes can see everything all of the time. The eyes of the carving were a comfort to someone, but if the carving was an idol, it would be bringing fear instead of comfort to just as many people."

"Very good, Kitten."

"But, Dad...?

"Yes?"

"I could have used another one. I was thinking of the one that says, 'Be not proud.' I can't remember how it's used in the Bible, but if I had made what Marita made, I would be very proud. Would that be a sin?"

"Well, Darla, I believe there are different kinds of pride. I believe in Marita's case, it would be pleasure of accomplishment instead of pride. And then we remember that 'every good and perfect gift comes from above'. The ability to carve can be considered a gift, and so would certainly have come from God. God gives strength and ability to create beauty. We even do some of that when we take pictures and bring them, through the television, to people who would never be able to come to places like this. Now, off to bed with you, all of you. It's getting late."

Morning came too soon. Darla's eyes would not open.

"Dad, I can't see anything. Everything looks dark."

"She doesn't even have her eyes open, Dad."

"Make her hurry and get up, Dad. I'm hungry."

Darla moaned, "Just a minute more, Dad. Please?"

"We could go off and leave her, Dad."

"I guess she isn't hungry."

"I think she wants granola bars for breakfast."

"Make her get up, Dad."

"Dad, can we get her up? I could throw a cup of cold water on her."

Mr. Wentworth stood surveying the lump under the bedcovers that was his daughter, and listened to the muffled sleepy sounds coming from the lump.

"Yeah, Dad, make her hurry," encouraged Dennis. "It takes her an hour to get the rat nests out of her hair."

"We'll die of starvation if we wait on her," pointed out Danny.

"All right, Kitten. You can sleep a little longer. I have to go send off my film and you can meet us at breakfast."

"Mmmmmm," came the grateful sound from under the bedspread.

"Oh, goodie. Come on, Danny, I'll race you."

The noise burst out of the door and down the hall and the door to room 204 closed softly. The only sound left in the room was the tick-tock of the travel clock.

Darla pulled the pillow over her head and sighed, but the sound of the quiet room and the ticking of the clock seemed to remind her that the family was gone without her. She was so accustomed to noise, that when it went away, she couldn't go back to sleep.

She sat up in bed, now wide awake. If she couldn't sleep, she might just as well get ready to go down to breakfast. She reached for her hair brush and was amazed that there were so few tangles. She must have hardly moved a muscle last night while she slept.

Suddenly, she was very hungry. She pulled on her jeans and shirt and went out the door into the hall. Dad and the boys should be eating breakfast by now.

Juan and Gilberto had watched the two boys burst out of the door and race down the hall, followed by the man. They turned to look at each other and they smiled when their eyes met. The job would be easy now.

The door opened, and they watched and waited. Then it closed again. When the girl came out, she would be alone. This was going to be as easy as shooting fish in a rain barrel.

Now they must decide. Should they wait by the door and risk the man coming back, or should they force their way into the room and risk having her scream like girls always do? While they were deciding, the door opened again and out stepped Darla.

Juan caught Darla's right arm and she turned, startled. Then he caught her other arm and held them both in his iron grip.

Darla opened her mouth to scream but a sticky plaster landed on her face. She pulled and jerked but the strong hands only held her tighter.

"Don't you be scared, little lady," Gilberto tried to assure her. "We won't be hurting you. We don't hurt girl children. We're going to help you get home."

Home? What was the matter with these men? But they wouldn't let her talk. She could only make a noise through her nose and even that sound was not very loud. They didn't seem to care that she wanted to speak.

They marched her down the stairway, making her walk between them. It was a tight squeeze, and then, at the lobby, Juan swung her up into his arms like he was carrying a baby and ran with her.

A uniformed man tried to stop them, but Juan shouted, "Sick. We got to get her to the hospital, quick. Run ahead and start the car, Gilberto."

Gilberto had already run ahead and the noisy motor of the car would have drowned any cry for help that Darla would have made. The plaster made her keep silent and she had already realized that it was useless to struggle. Together they were a lot stronger than she was.

Juan sat in the back seat holding her arms behind her while Gilberto drove, racing, though the narrow streets. This would have been a good time for the police to stop them, Darla thought, but there were no uniforms in sight.

At the door of a large white house they stopped, and Juan was still holding her tightly. She was pushed along the sidewalk toward the door which was opened by a man in an expensive suit and silk shirt. Inside the door, two other men pulled her away from Juan and in a minute the noisy motor of the car told Darla her captors were driving away.

Juan looked at the money in his hand. "Not bad for five days of work," he gloated, as he handed Gilberto his share. "But there is something about that little girl that didn't seem quite right to me."

"What do you mean?" Gilberto asked as he pocketed the money.

"Number one thing, she did not seem to know that man in the dandy shirt. Then they didn't take the plaster off, and they shoved her in the other room. If she was knowing the man, would she act that way?"

"That's not for us to know. Who can figure what goes on the mind of a girl child."

"Still...." muttered Juan, but his words were drowned by the sound of the motor.

Mr. Silk Shirt, whose name was Charles Manford, said to his associate, "So far, so good, Phillip. This plan was a good one. I'll have to give you credit for that. If there is any airplane that could escape being searched at the border, it would belong to that globe-trotting photographer."

Phillip Darcy nodded. "I know it was good plan. I did my homework well. That man will do whatever we ask him to do, just to get this youngen back. I'll go give him a call right now and get the project moving."

Dennis and Danny had ordered breakfast and were busily eating when their father joined them, after sending his film. Darla was still not there.

Mr. Wentworth decided that yesterday's activities must have really worn her out. He'd just go ahead and eat with the boys, and that would give her a little longer to sleep. They could just take something with them for her to eat on the way.

He was just about finished with his breakfast when the Public Addess System of the hotel announced a telephone call for Mr. Monty Wentworth. *Hmmmm*, who would be calling him at this time of the day? Only his family back in Branson, Missouri, and his customer in Kansas City knew exactly where he was staying. There must be a change in assignment or something. He picked up the phone.

"Monty Wentworth here."

"Mr. Wentworth, we have your little girl," came the words that exploded in his mind like a rocket.

"Who are you?"

"It doesn't matter who we are. We won't hurt her and we'll be glad to give her back to you but first you must do something for us."

"I don't believe you have her," bluffed the father.

"Do you want to hear her voice? HEY, BRING IN THE GIRL! Here, kid, say something to your daddy so he'll believe we have you."

"Dad?"

"Kitten, where are you?"

"I don't know, Daddy, but two men grabbed me and the...." Her voice was muffled, then silent.

"Mr. Wentworth, do you believe us now?"

Above his pounding heart, he answered, "What do you want me to do?"

"It's very simple, really," came the answer. "We want you to go home to Branson, Missouri. There is a suitcase with something of ours which we want you to take to Branson and leave at the address on the package. When you do that, you can have your youngen back. Just consider it a job of airmail transport and the pay will be getting your daughter back again."

The photographer was forcing his mind to think fast. These men meant business! "Did you say the package is in my plane? How did you get it in there?"

"Never mind that. We also have your plane bugged and we can track you anywhere so don't try to be funny and do something like notifying the police. Someone will be trailing you all the time and we can get one of those boys of yours as easily as we got the girl. Do you understand?"

"Yes, but there's just one thing. I have a crate to be delivered to the city library. Wouldn't it seem strange if I took it back to Missouri with me? Wouldn't that attract the police?"

There was a pause on the line. They must be talking it over. "All right. You go ahead and deliver the crate but you hurry! Don't try to get a message to anyone and if you do, we'll know it. Remember, we have that cute little girl of yours right here with us!"

Monty Wentworth's mind raced, trying to put together a plan. "Where can I reach you to pick her up?"

"You can't," came the answer. "We'll reach you if we need to say anything. That little bundle in your airplane is worth a billion dollars to us. How much is this kid worth to you? Just remember that if you try to cross us up."

"A billion is about what she's worth to me," admitted the photographer. "I'll do as you say."

"Then get cracking and don't mess up." Then came the dial tone as the man hung up the phone. For a few seconds he stood there, staring at the phone in his hand.

"Hey, Dad, shall I go get Darla now?"

"What's wrong, Dad? Was it bad news?"

"Boys," he said softly, "Darla's been kidnapped."

"Kidnapped? Why?"

"Was that the call about the ransom money?"

"What are we going to do?"

"How much do they want?"

"Can we get enough?"

"Shall we call the police?"

The father looked from one to the other of the boys. "I have to think. Just be quiet for a minute."

"But, Dad?"

Two sets of brown eyes watched him, silently.

"Boys," he said finally, "I tried to think fast and buy us time to get a message to someone but they told me we were being watched all of the time. We have to be very careful."

"Someone is watching us right now?"

"Boys, we'll have to assume there is. We must act carefully, so they won't do anything to Darla. Now, I told them we had to deliver a crate to the library."

"Crate of what?"

"I didn't know anything about it."

"He didn't either, Dennis. He's trying to think up a plan."

"Oh."

The man sighed. "I don't know if the plan will be any good. It isn't worked out in my mind, yet. I thought I could use that time to get a message to Tony Cervantas over at the library, but now I can't risk it. I'll have to think some more."

Just at that moment, the Public Address System announced another phone call for Mr. Wentworth.

"Hello?"

"It's me again," came the voice of the kidnapper. "We are watching you while you talk and whatever it is you're planning, just forget it. Leave those boys in the airplane when you deliver the crate. We'll know it if you don't. Like I told you a while ago, we are watching you all the time. Now do you believe it?" There as a click and a dial tone.

Mr. Wentworth turned to the boys. "They really are watching us this minute, but I think they gave me an idea. Let's go back to the room. Walk slow and we can make plans on the way because they certainly have the room bugged."

The boys plodded along behind their father as they walked up the stairs.

"Here's the plan," their dad said softly. "It is not a good one but it is the only one I can think of right now. I need two helpers. One has to be very brave and able to hold his breath for a long time and the other one has to be quick with the words and able to think and talk fast. Which is which?"

The boys looked at each other. They each took a deep breath and held it. The three people were silent until Danny was forced to breathe. Dad nodded. "Dennis goes in the crate and Danny does the talking."

"Crate? What crate?"

"What do I have to talk about? Who do I talk to?"

"I'll explain." They were up the stairs now, and walking down the hall. He must hurry. "The only chance we have to get a message to Tony at the library is for Dennis to deliver it. That way we can be sure it gets to him. We won't know what person is watching us so we will have to suspect everyone. I will deliver the crate and Dennis will be in it."

"What crate?" Dennis asked again.

"The food crate from the Beechking," his father explained. "I think you will be able to get inside of it. If not, we're in trouble."

Dennis scrunched his shoulders together to make himself smaller. "I wish I hadn't eaten so much breakfast."

"Oh, I don't think that would make any difference," assured his father.

"It isn't that. It's just that I think I'm getting sick because I'm so scared."

"No, Dennis. Forget it. You're not going to get sick because we haven't that much time."

"All right, Dad."

Monty Wentworth was tossing Darla's things into her suitcase, wondering if she would ever be needing them again. Kidnapping a person as old as Darla was very serious. They could always identify their captors and the kidnappers usually considered it safer for themselves if they...well, anyway, he'd gather up her things and put them in a suitcase.

Danny stood by, helplessly. "Dad, who am I going to talk to?" he whispered. "It isn't Tony, is it?"

"No, Danny," his dad answered, also in a whisper. "You will be talking to yourself. That second call said to leave you boys in the airplane and that it was bugged so they would know if we didn't. You are going to say things to Dennis and them answer them yourself. They don't know your voices and you will just have to make it sound like there are two boys in the plane."

"What things do I say, Dad?"

"You'll just have to think up something. I'm counting on you, son, now pack up your suitcase and hurry."

The car from the hotel took them to the airport where the Beechking waited.

"Hurry back," the driver invited them in a friendly way.

Mr. Wentworth told him goodbye. Was he one of the watchers? Probably. Or it could have been one of the mechanics who worked on the plane, filling it with gas and such. Surely, they would be involved somehow in order to get a "bugging" device into the Beechking. How about the control tower? Someone there could be the spy. ANYBODY could be the spy!

In the airplane he motioned to the boys for silence. They stowed away the gear, speaking only about casual things. "Shall we put all the suitcases together?" "Help me slide the crate around," and other such statements.

Dennis watched as his father scribbled a note. "Breathe slowly and carefully and push up on the lid a little so more air can get in. When you hear Tony's voice, jump out and tell him everything. Then you stay with him and try to help him in any way you can."

Dennis emptied the contents of the wooden food crate and stepped into it. He squirmed all the way down inside, lying on his back with his knees on his chest. He nodded that he was ready, and his dad closed the lid and fastened the clasp.

Mr. Wentworth used a little four wheeled flat cart to move the crate out of the airplane. Any package going to the library would probably contain books so it was not unreasonable that it would be heavy. He had called for a truck from the library to come for the cargo.

"What cargo?" the contact at the library asked. "We expected no cargo."

"But this is something Mr. Cervantes ordered. Send the truck quickly because I haven't much time." He used his stern, 'I want this done right now' voice, and it worked.

"Certainly, Senor. The truck will be on the way."

And it was. The truck driver was in no hurry. (Was he also one of the watchers?) Who could be sure? But they finally got to the library.

"We'll give you a receipt for the cargo," the receptionist told him but Mr. Wentworth refused.

"No. This is very valuable, and I must see that Mr. Cervantes has it right now. I'll see to it, myself." Whereupon he began to push the crate down the hall.

"No! No! You cannot do that!" the receptionist called, running after him.

But the photographer did not stop. He pushed the crate down the hall to the office he knew belonged to his friend.

Tony Cervantes looked up, smiling. He started to get up from the desk to greet him, but a look from Monty Wentworth stopped him. "Senor Cervantes," he said, "Here are the objects you ordered."

"Come on in," Tony invited him hesitantly. What was going on?

"Oh, no, Senor," insisted Monty. "We may not take tips."

Now Tony knew he was part of a game. He played along. "Then, thank you so much, friend."

Mr. Wentworth hurried back down the hall and called to the receptionist to follow. "I need that receipt and be quick. I must be on my way."

Receipt in hand, he hurried away, leaving Dennis to tell the story. So far, so good.

Tony Cervantes, manager of the Government Library in Mexico City, watched as his long time friend retreated down the hall. Then he stepped back into his office, puzzled. He looked at the crate and nudged it gently with his toe. A knock-knock came from within the crate and he jerked back. Then he reached carefully down and lifted the lid.

"Merciful heaven!" he exclaimed, as a boy popped out of the box.

Darla was no longer wearing the plaster over her mouth but she knew there would be no reason to scream. No one who could help her would be close enough to hear her. The door to the room was locked and there were bars on the only window. They had put a chain around one wrist, attaching her to a doorknob, leaving just enough slack in the chain for her to reach the adjoining bathroom. Obviously, they intended for her to be staying there a long time.

She had not heard much of the conversation with her dad over the telephone, but she did hear something about a billion dollars. If that was the ransom they were asking for her, she would never be released. There was no possible way her dad could find that much money.

Her heart pounded and she was sick at her stomach. Certainly she would never see her family again. If they were in the States, the police would be able to help, but Mexico was a foreign country. Would they help? Probably not.

A billion dollars! Why, there was probably not that much money in the whole town of Branson, Missouri! Dad would have to sell the plane and that even that would not be enough. And how long would it take him? And, just think, it all had happened because she got up late for breakfast.

Danny walked around in the Beechking, just in case someone was watching. He had to look like two boys. He walked by the window, then dropped to the floor and crawled backward, so he could walk by the window again. It was a good thing they looked alike...this way they could substitute for each other. Anyone who was watching would see a boy at this window and a boy at that window.

"Dennis?" he said to the empty airplane.

"What?" he answered himself. If he was being monitored, it would be all right to talk about the kidnapping. After all, it had been done right in front of him and Dennis.

"I'm scared," he told himself truthfully.

"Me, too. What do you think is going to happen?"

"I don't know. I just wish Dad would hurry and get back from the library."

Danny turned his head from side to side when he changed 'persons.' He didn't try to change his voice. Twins (or triplets) had a right to sound alike, didn't they? And besides, these people had never heard him or Dennis speak. Or had they? Where did they put that 'bug,' anyway?

As he walked around, talking to 'Dennis,' he looked for the hidden microphone, but he didn't see it. He couldn't afford to look too carefully, and if he found it, he couldn't remove it. He had to pretend nothing was being done to rescue Darla. Was there?

"Sit down, Danny," he told himself.

"I can't. I'm too nervous," he answered.

"But stomping around here isn't going to help."

"It might. I might trip on something and fall down and hit my head. If I was unconscious I would not be so scared."

"Where do you think Dad is right now?"

"He's probably at the library. I think he has the crate unloaded and is on his way back. No, I don't know where he is. I just wish he would hurry."

"Why?"

"Because we need to hurry back to Branson."

"Hush up talking. I think I'm going to cry."

"Me, too."

Would the hidden mike, wherever it was, be able to tell there was only one person crying? Maybe he shouldn't risk it.

"Hush up, Dennis. We can't let ourselves cry. Crying will only make it worse."

Danny sniffed loudly. "I'll try."

Danny was getting tired of making conversation. "Turn on the CD, Dennis. Maybe music will make us feel better."

Danny snapped on the CD and Dad's music filled the plane. Then Danny settled down in the depth of Dad's pilot seat and listened. *Hurry, Dad, I don't know what to do next.*

Darla sat on the unmade bed and looked at the walls of her bedroom prison. Finally her heart had stopped pounding and the tears had stopped forming in her eyes. She needed to make plans. The sound of voices came from another part of the house but they were too faint to tell what was going on. She couldn't even make out any of the words.

She had to get out. Dad and the boys had no idea where she was. She was holding up the filming schedule and where would they get enough money to pay the ransom?

She looked in the chest of drawers but she didn't know what she was hoping to find. Anyway, she didn't find it. There was nothing in the closet, either. There was no one and nothing. She was all alone. *God, are You in here with me? Remember, You promised not to leave me, but I'm afraid. Where are You?*

Later in the day someone handed her a hamburger through the partly opened door and she took it. She wasn't particularly hungry but when would she get something else? So she ate it. She drank water form the faucet in the bathroom using her hands as a cup.

Then she sat down and waited.

What else could she do, locked in a room with bars on the window with her wrist chained to the door? She could do a lot of thinking, that's what she could do. *Help me think, God. I've just got to get out of here.*

Back in the library, Dennis took a deep breath, glad to be free of the crate. The man backed away from the crate with eyes round as saucers.

"You! Aren't you Monty's kid? What are you doing here? That crate....Where did your daddy go in such a hurry? Tell me, what is going on?"

"Dad had to leave because they're watching us. You've got to help us. They've got Darla!"

"Darla? Your sister? Who has her?"

"Kidnappers. They called Dad."

"How much money do they want?"

"They don't want money, Mr. Cervantes. They want Dad to smuggle something back across the border for them."

"What?"

"It's in a suitcase in the airplane. It was locked."

"Hmmm, where is your dad?"

"Gone home. They told him to go to Branson. I was supposed to ask you to do something."

"What was I supposed to do?"

"I don't know. Dad didn't have time to figure anything out but they said he could get Darla when he delivered the suitcase to the address in Missouri, so he took off."

"Well, he won't."

"Huh? Won't what?"

"He won't get Darla. She will be out of the city by that time, if I don't miss my guess."

"But...."

"Hush a minute, son. We've got to think. A suitcase, you said? They either have drugs or stolen art. I'd say it was art because that way they would know of your dad. Yes, that would be it. They would be trying to smuggle paintings or something. Oh, I know! It would be the gem stones and jewels for the display."

"Where would they get the gem stones? We only took pictures of carvings. We didn't even get down to Guatemala yet. That's where the gems were."

"Hmmm. Were you followed, uh...which one are you? Danny?"

"No, I'm Dennis. If we were followed, we didn't notice it, but then, we weren't looking, either."

"Sure. I don't think that's what happened, because it doesn't sound like a spur-of-the-moment kidnapping. Somehow they got information about your schedule or they wouldn't have been able to plan it so well."

"What shall we do?"

"Let me think. Something would have to be very valuable to be worth all of this trouble."

"Pictures? That's all we had."

"No, they weren't after what you had. They just want to get something across the border. Stolen gems, that's what it would be."

"What do we do now?"

"First we alert Missouri law enforcement to watch for the plane and tail your Dad when he makes the delivery."

"Oh, don't do that! They said not to tell the police or they would kill Darla."

"How old is Darla, Son?"

"Thirteen, the same as I am."

Mr. Cervantes nodded, sadly. "And she's old enough to identify someone who kidnapped her. They do not plan to let her go, no matter what we do."

"What will they do to her?"

"Dennis, let's don't waste time talking. You sit down there while I make the call. We need to get the police started, then we'll find Darla."

"We will?" Dennis really wanted to believe him but Mexico City was very large. Still....

After the call, Dennis and the man went back to the hotel where they had been staying. It was always best to start at the beginning.

"Did you see anyone? Anyone at all who seemed interested in you?"

"No, Sir...Danny and I were busy eating. We don't look around much because a lot of people seem to notice us. Being triplets, I guess, makes them more interested in staring at us."

"Well, don't worry, Dennis. We'll think of something. It's a strange fact, but people, or actually criminals, usually go back to the scene of the crime and if we hurry, we might find something that will help us."

Gilberto and Juan parked their noisy car in front of the hotel.

"Why do you want to come back here?" Juan asked. "We did our job and we can go on."

"Later, amigo. I just hankered after a little breakfast and what folks were eating here was looking good to me when I had no money. Now we got us money and I got a big hunger setting down inside me. Sitting around watching and thinking always did make me hungry."

"But why here?"

"No reason not to be here. No one saw us, and besides, we didn't really do anything wrong."

"The people in the lobby saw us when we carried her out."

"But you told them a good lie. They thought we was good guys. Maybe we were." Gilberto chuckled softly.

"Yeah, and I thought we were then. Now I ain't so sure. Things ain't adding up right. That little girl didn't want to go."

"I noticed that, too. You think maybe we was lied to?"

"I don't know what to think. Let's have us some coffee."

The two men sat down at a table in the restaurant.

"I keep thinking about that little girl."

"Yeah, and I'm not so happy, either. I think we done the wrong thing."

"But how are we going to know?"

"We're not."

"We could drive back out there."

"What good would that do? They may be gone with her by now." Gilberto looked at the hotel restaurant menu and realized he was not as hungry as he thought he was.

"Just a cup of coffee," he requested.

Just at that moment a man and a half grown boy came into the room. The man looked around and then came toward Juan and Gilberto.

"Gentlemen?" the man greeted them.

Gilberto looked behind himself to see the gentleman this man was talking to but Juan nudged him with his foot.

"It's us he's talking to," he whispered.

"Gentlemen," the man repeated. "I find myself in need of a little help."

"You wanting to hire us for a job, mister? We're strong." Two jobs were always better than one and the money they had earned today would not last forever. Juan indicated that the man and boy should sit down at their table.

Gilberto agreed. "We're strong. Together we can get most things done."

The man sat down. "Gentlemen, it is not your muscles I need to hire."

"Huh? What then?"

"Your eyes!"

"Eyes? No one ever hired our eyes before."

"But I want to," the man insisted. "A couple of intelligent gentlemen like you two would remember if you saw something unusual happen while you were sitting here drinking your coffee."

They nodded.

"Were you here this morning?" the man asked.

The two men were silent. It was always better to say nothing than to risk saying the wrong thing. Just then the half grown kid took off his hat and the tousled, honey-colored hair came into sight.

Juan nudged Gilberto again. This was one of the boys they had been following. But this was not the same man. Uh, oh...trouble was about to happen. Was this the law?

"Mister, whatever it is you want, we don't know nothing. We just drove up in our car just this minute," Gilberto explained. "Ask anyone. Ask that man at the door out in the lobby. He'll say that."

Tony Cervantes looked toward the door at the uniformed doorman, then at Gilberto, and Gilberto realized he had made a mistake. The doorman was the one who had tried to stop them. He would be only too glad to tell everything he saw. Especially if he saw the twenty dollar bill that Mr. Cervantes was fingering in his hand.

The man and the boy got up to go. "Thanks," the man told them. "I will go ask the man at the door."

"Wait!" called Juan and Gilberto, together. The man and the boy came back and sat down.

Juan offered, "Say what it is you want to know and we might remember."

Tony Cervantes put the twenty dollar bill on the table. "Here's what I need. A friend of mine with his three children came here on a business trip and someone kidnapped his little girl. They want to trick him into taking something out of the country for them."

"Really?"

Juan and Gilberto looked at each other. "We might have seen something that would help you."

"Yeah, we could have seen someone do something."

"When did it happen?"

"Oh, it was very early this morning."

"Really? You saw someone kidnap the little girl?"

Juan nodded. "Seen that for sure. They took that little girl right out of here. Yellow headed, she was, just like that boy, there."

Gilberto put in, "Could be, though, that them men was misled and thought they was doing that girl a favor. Or something."

Dennis sighed and looked from one to the other of the men. *Hurry up,* his mind told them. *Say what you have to say so we can go do something.* But Tony did not seem to be in a hurry. He talked simply and casually, just like there was no serious problem. He nodded as he agreed with the men.

"That's just about the way I figured it," Tony told them. "It's easy to get the wrong idea when you don't know all the facts." Another twenty dollar bill appeared on the table. Tony went on. "Would you, by any chance, know where that girl was taken?"

Gilberto glanced at the money. "Could be we would know something about that."

Tony nodded and waited.

Gilberto added, "We did see for sure the way they left when they went out of here."

"I was hoping you did."

"Yeah," put in Juan. "They took off down beside the river."

"Couldn't be too sure, though, how far they went." Gilberto added cautiously.

"Too bad," Tony said, shaking his head sadly. The fingers of his left hand causally picked up the last twenty dollar bill he had put on the table. "It sure would have helped to know how far they went. It would cut down on the time we must spend looking."

They sat in silence for a few minutes and another twenty dollar bill appeared in Tony's hand. He fingered the bills casually, smoothing and creasing them with his fingers. Forty American dollars!

Gilberto stroked his chin. "Mister, could be that we could make a guess where the exact place is that they took that girl."

Tony spread the forty dollars on top of the twenty dollars already on the table and nodded.

Juan pushed back his chair. "Gil, we need to be going anyway, and we was going down the river road. These here fellows would be welcome to follow us."

Tony and Dennis stood up encouragingly. Juan and Gilberto also stood up and Gilberto's hand casually scooped up the money and crammed it into his pocket.

Juan motioned to Dennis and Tony to follow him. "You fellows can follow on after us and we'll take you to the place where that little girl was took. Least ways, we think it was there."

The Beechking Aircraft climbed into the clouds and headed north. At the Gulf of Mexico, the silver-blue water shimmered beneath them but Monty Wentworth and Danny did not look down to admire its beauty.

Danny was staring out the window at the clouds outside the window beside him. It felt strange to be alone with Dad, without even Dennis around. What if they didn't get Darla back? What if she was killed? What if Dennis couldn't get help? What if Dennis got caught? Why did this happen? God must have forgotten that this family was one who believed in Him and trusted Him. Here they were, Christians, and God was letting this happen. *God, where in the world are You?*

Danny leaned toward the window and looked down at the water below him. A small ship inched its way across the water, creating a tiny wake. He looked up, past the clouds, and there was only more blue sky. *God, where are you? I have things to say to You, face to face. Man to Man....Human to God. Where are You, God?*

Then, in the stillness of the airplane, Danny heard within his mind. *What would you say to Me if you saw Me?*

Well, first I would ask why You let things get out of hand like this. And then I'd say, don't You like us anymore? Dad is so worried he can't think of a thing to say. He just stares straight ahead.

Yes, Danny, I still know about you.

Danny looked around quickly. No one was there.

Danny, I love you just like I loved Daniel when he was in the lion's den and like I loved the three young Hebrew men when they refused to worship the idol and were thrown into the fiery furnace.

Yeah, that's right God. You even went down there into the furnace with them and kept them from getting burned, didn't you, God?

Yes, Danny and I am right here with you, just like I was with them.

The voice was so plain and clear. Danny looked slowly around again, slowly, even though he knew no one was in the plane.

But, God, are you trying to tell me that everything is going to be all right?

Remember something I said to you, Danny. Pretend it is evening devotion and you are remembering my words to say to each other. If it was evening right now, what would you say?

Danny thought. *Here it is, God. I'd say, "All things work together for the good to them that love God." I love you, God. You know that. We all love You. But tell me, how can all of this be good?*

Danny, that is not a question you have to answer. Dennis may not have time to think about Me right now. What would you like to think of for him? What words would you want him to say to Me?

That's easy, God. I'd say, "Thy word is a lamp unto my feet and a light unto my pathway." I really want you to show me what I need to do.

And Darla? What would you say for her?

I know one for her, too, God. You said You were with us always, even unto the ends of the earth. This is certainly one part of the earth. Maybe it's not the end of the earth, but anyway, I am glad You're here with me.

Now, Danny, do you know where I am?

Yes, God, You're right here. I'm sorry I ever doubted.

Danny looked toward his father. His dad's face looked like it had been carved from wood. It was firm and hard and his dark brown eyes stared ahead, unblinkingly, into the blue of the sky. Danny sighed but he didn't say anything.

The Beechking Aircraft crossed over the border near Laredo, Texas. The pilot picked up the radio mike. "Beechking ICU2. Mexico City to Springfield, Missouri. Just passing through. Over and out."

"Roger, Beechking ICU2. Happy landing."

The Air Traffic Controller at Laredo called to the shift supervisor. "The aircraft with the contraband just passed over. Would you alert the Air Base at San Antonio to pick them up on radar?"

Dennis rode beside Tony Cervantes as they followed Juan and Gilberto.

"One thing I can't understand," he told Tony.

"What's that?"

"If those men saw the kidnapping from the lobby, how did they know where Darla was taken if they didn't follow the kidnappers? Do you think we may be driving into a trap?"

"No, Dennis. These two men were the very ones who took Darla."

"These? And you knew it? Why didn't you call the police?"

Tony explained, "If I did, then the men would say they knew nothing, just like they did when we first asked them. This way, they can save face, they won't be caught, and they get the money. I think they were telling the truth when they said they didn't realize what they were doing. After all, what we really want is Darla, isn't it?"

Dennis nodded. He bit his lip and realized it was very sore from the last time he bit it.

The old car led them down a dirty road where the houses became farther apart. They honked the car horn and Juan pointed to a white house set back off the road. Then he waved to them and turned off on a side road.

Without slowing down, Tony honked his car horn in response, and kept driving, passing in front of the row of houses. Danny looked at the front and the side of the house. A car and a pickup were parked in the yard and there were lights on in several rooms.

"I think she's still there," he decided.

"I agree," said Tony, as he turned a corner and parked by a grove of trees. "The big problem is, which room is she in?"

"Aren't we going to call the police?"

"Can we afford the time, Dennis?"

"I guess not. I could sneak up there and peek in the windows."

Tony was silent, rubbing his chin in thought. "Yes, that might work."

Dennis had reached for the car door latch, but Tony stopped him. "Wait." He scrounged around in the back seat until he located a short rope. "If anyone challenges you, or asks what you're doing, ask them if they have seen a little dog. Then you have to be ready to describe a dog...any dog you remember."

Dennis took the rope and started back toward the houses, slipping through the grove of trees and a lot of small bushes. There were vines and clumps of shrubbery and it was easy to stay hidden until he came close to the house.

Darla would be in the back of the houses, he was sure. He slipped through the bushes to a back room. The window was dark, but the one around the corner had a light on. He picked up a tiny rock and tossed it toward the house, but it fell short.

He crept closer and picked up another pebble. It popped against the wood siding and bounced back. He waited...still nothing.

He tried again and this time he saw something move inside the room. Someone leaned against the window and then jumped back. Darla! She was there!

Dennis dashed the short distance to the window and threw himself on the ground just below it. He waited a minute, then eased himself up. Darla was leaning against the window as though to block the view. Dennis could now see the bars on the window...thick metal bars attached to the wood of the window with screws. Screws! Good! What he needed was a screwdriver.

He dashed back to the trees. The mongrel dog across the street saw movement and began to bark. Should Dennis run now that the dog was making this much noise? Or would the dog chase after him? Which...? *Sneak, Dennis,* he told himself. *That would be the safer way.*

The dog was noisy and it looked directly at Dennis, so he sneaked faster. He was breathless when he reached the car.

"I have to have a screwdriver. The window has bars on it."

"You saw her?"

"Yes, and she saw me but she can't get out through the window. I need the screwdriver."

"No, Dennis, I need to go do it."

"But I know just what has to be done. Please, I want to do it!"

"But, Dennis, your light hair really shows up in a country of dark haired people."

Dennis ignored him. "Hurry, please. I have to get back."

"Did you see her for sure?"

"I sure did."

"Is she alone in the room?"

"I don't know about that. She was leaning against the window."

"Then I would think she wasn't alone and she was trying to keep whoever was with her from seeing you. You'll have to be very careful."

"Quick! I need the screwdriver."

Tool in hand, Dennis crawled back through the bushes, trying not to attract the attention of the dog again. Instead of dashing from the trees to the house, he wriggled across the grass on his elbows. Then he raised up slowly and pushed the screwdriver through the mesh of the screen. He was lucky. It just fit the screws.

Carefully, he eased one screw loose...then the other end. The bottom bar came loose and it fell with a quiet 'chunk' to the bottom of the window.

Darla still leaned against the glass. He would have to be very quiet.

Another problem. The bottom bar didn't make much noise when it fell but the top one would. When it fell to the bottom of the window against the one that was already there, it would make a loud 'clang.'

What shall I do, God?

The idea came. *Ah, I'll just loosen one end and push it down. Darla isn't very big. She can get through a very small place.*

The Air Traffic Controller in Waco, Texas, told his mike, "Acknowledge Beechking ICU2. Have a good day."

Then to the shift supervisor he reported, "Tell Dallas World Airport the jet is ahead of schedule. That pilot must be trying to get this over with as soon as he can. It might be time to notify Fort Smith, Arkansas, too, at the speed they're traveling."

Dennis loosened one end of the top bar and pushed it down with the screwdriver. It was then he heard the metallic 'clink' against the window glass. There, on Darla's wrist, was a chain. It clattered loudly against the window. Then it banged three times. A signal! For what?

Dennis eased down below the window and crept back to the backside of the house. He could hear footsteps inside the room and he heard a man's voice. Was Dennis too late? Were they taking her away right now?

Then it became quiet again and he slipped back to the window. He eased the window screen off the window and put it on the ground.

Darla was still leaning against the glass. Her fingers eased under the window and raised it an inch.

"Screwdriver!" she whispered.

Dennis poked the screwdriver into her hand and slipped back around the house. The window closed again.

Dennis pressed himself against the house and waited, afraid to breathe. How long should he wait? Should he go get Tony? *Help me, God.*

Then he heard voices again. He heard a door close, then open, then close again.

When, God?

He slipped back around to the window. Oh, she was still there! Her fingers were under the bottom of the window.

"Help me!" she whispered. "It's stuck!"

As Darla lifted from the inside of the window, Dennis lifted from the outside, but the ancient, much painted window was stuck. It would go no higher than seven or eight inches.

Dennis lay down on the ground and lifted one foot, placing it firmly against the bottom of the window. With a sharp kick from the other foot, he unstuck the window, causing a loud bang and crackling of paint which flew in every direction. One pane of glass loosened itself from the rotted putty and fell away from the window. It hit with a clang and a crash against the metal bars of the window and tinkled into a million slivers all around him.

Darla lost no time and came crawling through the window like a monkey out of a crate and landed on top of Dennis where he lay on the ground.

She jumped to her feet and pulled Dennis up with her. "Hurry! They're coming back."

Amid the frantic barking of the dog, Dennis and Darla ran through the woods.

From behind them came loud angry voices and the sound of a car motor. Then the motor of the pickup roared into life and came rumbling down the road. They threw themselves on the ground behind a grass clump as it roared past.

They caught sight of Tony's car. Trouble! It was firmly wedged between the car and pickup of the camper, and they were questioning Tony.

Dennis and Darla squirmed forward to a thicket of trees. They could hear the voices of the men asking Tony why he was here and if he saw a girl come down the road.

No, Tony had told them, truthfully. He had seen no girl all day. But he did see something.

"What did you see?" they asked.

"This little spider," the boy and girl heard Tony say. "Do you men know that this little spider is so important that it was written up in a naturalist journal? When these spiders hatch, they make a long web and float on the wind for miles and miles. They have even landed on ships at sea. Isn't that amazing?"

One of the men said, "Aw, let's go. This nut doesn't know anything."

They walked away but Dennis and Darla heard Tony call after them, "I may be a nut, but I knew about the spider. Does that count?"

The men didn't bother to answer.

The airport at Fort Smith, Arkansas, picked up the Beechking on their radar.

"Acknowledge Beechking ICU2. Remain in holding pattern for instructions."

The pilot of the Beechking picked up his mike. "Acknowledge, Fort Smith Tower."

In a minute the radio came on again. "Fort Smith Tower to Beechking ICU2. We have a runway problem. Do you have fuel to divert to Will Rogers World Airport, Oklahoma City?"

"This is Beechking ICU2. Affirmative. Request permission to go on to Will Rogers World Airport."

"Tower to Beechking ICU2. Permission granted and thanks. Tower out."

Danny leaned over to the window and looked down. The runways were clear and air traffic was light. Somehow Dad didn't seem to question the strange instructions. Danny opened his mouth to ask why, but decided against it.

Where are You, God? Why didn't You let us come down?

Think, Danny. "All things work together for the good to them that love Me."

I'm sorry, God.

And neither Danny nor his father saw the other plane divert, and follow them on to the Oklahoma City Airport.

As Dennis and Darla watched from the shrubbery, Tony started the car motor and eased away. The boy and girl looked at each other in dismay, their hearts pounding.

The kidnappers? The dog? The daylight? The strange town? What were they going to do now and why did Tony leave them?

The dog stopped barking and there were no more cars on the little road. What now? Where would the safest place be? Should they run, or would the kidnappers think that was what they would do? Should they stay where they were? But what about the dog?

And Darla still had a length of chain on her wrist.

"You pried open a link on that chain with the screwdriver?" Dennis whispered, amazed.

Darla nodded. "It was the loosest one. I had been looking for something to pry with, and then you got there with the screwdriver."

Nearby them on the ground was an ant hill, and the insects had found their legs and had begun to sting. The fiery bites helped them to decide to leave their hiding place.

"We've got to move!"

"Where to? I'm afraid to go far. Tony won't know where we are."

"But the ants are eating us up!"

Then they heard the motor of the kidnappers's pickup. It was coming slowly down the road. There were voices back at the house, and they were calling instructions to each other and yelling.

Darla rubbed the stinging ants from her leg, and whispered, "Come on, Dennis. We've got to run. They'll be beating the bushes for me in a few minutes...."

They scurried across the road, crouching low. There were no cars in sight.

"Come on! Hurry!"

Their shoes against the rocks on the road seemed to make a loud noise. Surely they could be heard all over Mexico! They threw themselves in the ditch and squirmed up the bank into a grove of avocado trees. The trees in the orchard were tall and cool-green but the trunks were too large to reach around. How would they be able to climb?

"But we have to get up," Darla complained.

"I have an idea. Toss the chain over the limb and I'll hold the end while you use it to climb up. Then you can hold it and help me."

"Dennis, I don't know if...."

"Do you have a better idea?"

"No."

"Then hurry and let me have the end of the chain. I'll throw it up over the limb."

Up and over the limb rattled the noisy chain, tugging at Darla's arm as it fell over the other side. Dennis held tightly to the end of the chain as Darla climbed up the clanging, swinging metal and reached for the limb. Then she twisted the chain around the limb a couple of times and held it while Dennis followed.

They scaled upward to the top of the tree and pulled up the long chain, wrapping it around a limb to keep it quiet.

Now, unless someone was very good at tracking footprints, they would never find them up here. Of course, that meant Tony could not find them, either.

"Dennis," Darla whispered. "Let me see that screwdriver. I want to get this chain off."

"Hold out your arm and I'll try." Dennis offered. He braced the tool against a limb and twisted the chain. One of the links separated a tiny bit.

"Here, let me try." Darla pushed and twisted and the link separated a little bit wider.

"Let me try again." Dennis twisted the heavy chain until his face was red and his knuckles were white. "There, Darla, try to force that link through the separation."

The link barely slipped through and the gap in the chain closed. Now Darla had a chain on her wrist with only two links hanging on it, and they had a separate chain of about twelve feet long.

The voices below them were plainer now. The kidnappers were looking carefully everywhere. They had crossed the road and had come into the avocado grove, walking around the trees directly below Dennis and Darla. One of the men pointed up into their tree.

"Look up there what I see."

"What do you see?" questioned the other man.

"Just look up. See...right there? The avocados are ripe."

"Cut it out," scolded the other man. "You're going to forget all about avocados when they find out we let that girl get away. Keep your head down and keep looking for footprints or something."

The men walked slowly through the trees. The hard-packed ground looked no different than it had before and if someone had run across it, it would be almost impossible to see where.

The dusty leaves in the tree made Dennis want to sneeze. He drew in his breath, but smothered his face with his hands and the sneeze died away.

A large greenish spider advanced toward Darla's arm, hesitated for a minute, then climbed onto one finger. Darla watched the spider but did not move. She was holding the metal chain carefully and quietly in both hands and she had no fingers available to thump the spider away. She watched it as it stepped off her finger and onto her thumb. It began to walk slowly along her arm. Up the sleeve it went and onto her collar. Then to her neck. It continued to walk up, its pointed feet tickling her cheek.

"Dennis!" she whispered softly.

The spider climbed to her nose. Dennis eased his hand carefully around the tree.

The spider was still on Darla's nose. She was trying to watch it and she felt her eyes cross. Then there seemed to be two spiders looking at her with their bulging eyes. Fright bumps began to pop up along her arm.

Dennis closed his finger and thumb, took careful aim and thumped the spider away. The last they saw of it, the spider was floating softly to the ground on the web it had just spun.

The kidnappers were now out of the avocado grove and were almost out of sight. Dennis and Darla breathed a little more easily. There was no other traffic along the road until a red, old-model sedan stopped beside the road. A Mexican woman got out of the car and looked this way and that. Was she part of the kidnappers? Darla had not seen her, but that really meant nothing. The pair in the tree remained motionless. They could barely see her through the leaves of the trees but they were afraid to move to get a better look.

Then the old woman began to call in a hoarse, crackly voice.

"Monty! Where are you, son? Monty, you answer me!"

Darla and Dennis looked at each other quickly. Monty was an unusual name for a Mexican boy. Also that was their father's nickname.

And, hey, that was no woman! That was Tony in a dress and wearing a wig! He was using their father's name as a signal. What did he want them to do now? They strained their ears to hear the instructions.

The voice came again. "Hurry up, Monty. Your father is on his way home and we must get here first. If you don't hurry and come here this instant, you are going to be in a lot of trouble."

That was it! The signal and the instructions! Down through the limbs they came, chain rattling. At the lower limb the chain was looped over and tied and it helped them get low enough to drop without danger of a sprained ankle or worse.

Like the wind through the trees, they ran to the red car with the wide open doors.

When they reached the car, Tony whispered, "Darla, get in the back and lay down. Dennis, you put on this stocking cap." Loudly, he said, "You get in that car this minute, Monty."

Then Tony climbed into the car, accelerated instantly and zoomed down the dusty road. He squealed around corners and swerved past other cars. Dennis held to the seat belt and Darla hugged the floorboard to keep from being flung about.

They didn't slow down until they reached the brick building of the library.

They ran to the door and down the hall to Tony's office. Tony grabbed a phone and dialed. Breathlessly, he told the Mexican Police,

"I have them. Both of them and no one is hurt. Have you located their father?"

He was assured, "We have the father located. We are so glad your plan worked and that you have the children. We'll radio the news to the Oklahoma City airport."

Danny and his dad flew for fifty minutes of worried silence. From the distance they could see the aircraft of all sizes circling over Will Rogers World Airport like flies over a honey jar, waiting for permission to land. Every sort of large passenger and cargo plane was in the air.

Monty Wentworth shook his head and sighed. He was really low on fuel by now and there was no way to know how long he would be flying in a holding pattern, waiting his turn to land.

He picked up the mike. "Beechking ICU2 to Will Rogers Tower. Come in tower."

A voice leaped out of the radio to them. "Will Rogers Tower to Beechking ICU2. Drop to 500 feet of altitude, proceed to runway three and come on in. Tower out."

The pilot of the Beechking drew in a startled breath. The Air Traffic Controller had made an error. They almost never made mistakes like this one but obviously they gave instructions that were not correct. Aircraft traffic was circling the field like vegetables being stirred in a soup bowl. It was not possible that they would be landed ahead of everyone else.

"Beechking ICU2 to Tower. Request repeat of landing instructions."

"Tower to Beechking ICU2. Proceed immediately to runway three. Drop altitude and come on in. We're waiting for you."

Well, it couldn't be much plainer that that. "Beechking ICU2 to Tower, Affirmative. We're coming down."

The small jet lowered itself into the maze of massive airplanes like a hummingbird into a flock of hawks. Runway three was clear and clean all the way to the terminal. The small jet lowered its nose and headed in. There was no way the pilot could have seen the jet which left the runway and zoomed into the air to track the plane that had followed them from Fort Smith.

As the wheels of the Beechking touched the ground, a police car with circling lights came onto the runway. When the plane stopped, a swarm of uniforms surrounded it. Monty Wentworth opened the door and the first blue suit who entered the plane demanded. "Where is it?"

"Where is what?"

"The parcel, bundle or whatever it is?"

Danny pointed to the suitcase.

The uniformed officer told his radio. "Description: Suitcase, imitation alligator. Oliver drab in color. Measure 10 inches by 22 inches by 36 inches. Over and out."

Danny and his dad stared, puzzled, at the uniformed officers.

The sergeant apologized, "Sorry to be so abrupt, Mr. Wentworth, but we have another Beechking in the air almost ready to land in Springfield, and we needed to know what kind of a parcel it must be carrying. Now we need you to come with us into the terminal so we can get the rest of the information. We will need the address off the suitcase so our men will know where to deliver the contraband."

"But...."

"Yes, Sir?"

"If you have the package and the address, am I also in Springfield?"

The sergeant grinned. "Yes, Sir, you are! We found an officer who looks almost exactly like you. We even have your two boys in the airplane. We had a lot of trouble finding boys who looked alike, they tell me, and the ones they have are not even brothers, but we felt two boys should be along or the smugglers might get spooked."

"But there's my daughter, Darla, you know. They have her now and they were willing to exchange her for the suitcase. Please tell your men to be careful."

The sergeant put his hand over his face. "Oh, forgive me, Mr. Wentworth. I should have advised you the minute I saw you that your daughter is safe. We do not have her yet but we know where she is."

"Where is she?" he demanded.

"In the library in Mexico City with a fellow named Tony Cervantes who manages the Mexico City Library System. The Mexico police tell us he assisted in a daring, dangerous rescue."

"Thank you, God," the photographer breathed.

"Danny," the sergeant said, "would you and your dad like to see what you've been carrying in the suitcase?"

"Sure!" agreed Danny. "Do you know what it is?"

"We think we do. We hope it is the carved gems from the vault of the museum in Mexico City."

"Really? How much is it really worth? Not actually a billion dollars, huh?"

"Oh yes. I'm sure it's worth that, if it was for sale, which it certainly isn't."

The suitcase lock was forced open and there, packed in a nest of foam plastic beads, were the gems, larger than Danny's fist. The gem stones had been carved into animals and into strange faces. Some of them were set with gems of a different kind. Green emerald eyes sparkled out of diamond faces. There were lavender animals, black onyx faces and other items made from the greenish aquamarine and blood red ruby stones. They shone like giant glass beads nestled in their Styrofoam packing.

"These gems have to go back to Mexico City. We'd like to send them with you if you are going directly back. Or we can bring your children here and put these on another flight."

Danny's father looked down at him and smiled. "What about it, Dan? Do we go back right now, or do we wait till morning? We'll be really late if we go on today."

Danny shrugged and returned the grin. "I've not nothing else to do, Dad, and I know you weren't really asking me. You were going to go back right now no matter what I said. So let's get going."

It was almost midnight when the Beechking nosed downward toward the lights of the airport at Mexico City.

"Beechking ICU2 to Mexico City Tower. Request landing instructions."

"Tower to Beechking ICU2. You are cleared for landing on Runway four."

Down through the heavy air traffic came the little Beechking jet, nosing its way ahead of the other circling planes. The wheels of the Beechking touched down and at that moment there came toward them the Mexican Police cars with lights rotating.

"There they are again, Dad, after their famous suitcase."

His dad nodded. "I guess we'll just have to give it to them."

"None too soon for me," Danny decided.

The Mexican Police took the suitcase and Danny and his dad rode to the terminal with them. Tony, Dennis and Darla were waiting. Dennis warned his father, "Watch out, Dad, Darla's in a crying mood. She's going to get tears all over you."

Faster than the strike of a serpent's head came Darla's fist.

"Ouch!" yelled Dennis, holding his arm in pain.

"Now let's see who's crying," Darla retorted.

At a late dinner, almost breakfast, Tony explained, "I knew about the theft of the gems and I was working on it when you pushed your kid into my office. We were sure all along that it was an inside job, planned to occur when those gems were taken from the vault with a lot of other things for you to photograph.

"The kidnappers thought they would buy some getaway time by involving you and thereby keeping the missing gems from being noticed. But, of course, there is never just one person involved in a theft of this size, and something this important is bound to be missed quickly. But we didn't even have a good lead until Dennis got there."

He looked at Dennis and Darla. "We had a really interesting day, didn't we, kids? Shall we try to top it tomorrow?"

"NO!" shouted everyone, as one voice.

"All right, then. But I have to go now and you kids need to be in bed," then Tony was gone.

Back in their room, Darla asked, "If we say a verse, Dad, which day will it be for? Yesterday or tomorrow?"

Dad thought a minute. "Did you talk with God, today?"

"Yes! Over and over!"

"Then we'll go to sleep now and we'll have verses tomorrow. Into the bed with you, and hurry."

It took another two days to do the photography of the gem carvings. Each piece had to be placed just right and each one was photographed from several angles. It took so long that Darla was able to finish reading all the library books she had brought along.

As they flew over the blue water of the Gulf of Mexico toward Springfield, Missouri, Dennis and Danny squabbled over the checker game like two pups fighting over the same dirty sock. The pilot listened to music on his CD and Darla watched the clouds outside the window.

"Where do we go next, Dad?"

"How would you like to take a picture of a koala?"

"Really, Dad? Australia? You're not just teasing? I've always wanted to go there."

From the rear of the plane came the shout, "Yippee! Australia!"

"Sit still, Dennis. Look what you did!"

"I didn't mean to."

"Yes, you did, because you were losing the game."

"I wasn't."

"You were."

"Well, you must have been loosing because I was winning."

"You weren't."

"I was."

"You weren't."

"How can you say that? I had more kings."

"But I had a good move in my mind."

"But it never got out of your mind into your hand."

"It was going to."

"Shut up! Dad, are we really going to Australia?"

"He said we were."

"He didn't, either."

"No, he didn't, did you Dad? He asked Darla if she wanted to take a picture of a koala. She could do that at the zoo."

"But that's not what he meant, did you, Dad?"

"It could have been. Are we going to take pictures of the zoo animals?"

"I've heard that kangaroos can be taught to box. I want to box with a kangaroo.:"

"I wish you would. Maybe it would knock some sense into you."

"If I had any more sense, I'd beat you at checkers every time instead of just most of the time."

"Then I'd have sense enough not to play with you anymore."

"That's enough, boys."

There was silence from the rear of the plane. Then, "Set up the board, Danny. We've got time for another game."

"Okay, but we'll have to hurry."

Monty Wentworth, Photographer, picked up the mike. "Beechking ICU2 to Springfield Tower. Request landing instructions."

"Tower to Beechking ICU2. Climb to 1500 feet and hold for advancing Trans World. We'll advise you when you are cleared to land. Tower out."

"Beechking ICU2 to Tower. Affirmative."

The small jet nosed itself up into the cloud and leveled, circling over the airport. The big liner slid under them and settled onto the runway.

"How long are we going to be up here, Dad?"

"I don't know, Danny. It looks like it will be a while."

"Dad?"

"Yes, Danny?"

"Is it too late to exchange Darla for that suitcase? When we had it aboard, we got down a lot quicker. Remember how they let us land is front of everyone else?"

Before his dad could answer, Danny yelled, "Darla, don't you come back here. Go back! Don't you punch me! DAD! MAKE HER COME BACK UP THERE WITH YOU!…OUCH!!!!"

FOOTSTEPS IN THE CANYON

BOOK 2
FIRE IN THE CANYON
&
THE DIARY

FIRE IN THE CANYON

The white and tan barred owl had built her nest in a brush pile that had been caused by a lightning-felled tree, and had raised three chicks. Today, the last chick had flown, so there was no more need for the nest. On feathery wings, the owl arose into the warm air of the early spring day.

She had a plan, and the plan was to find a better place for her nest next year.

The brush pile was rotting down and by next year the nest would be too low to the ground to be safe. A ground nest was fine, but there was always a danger of a ferret, raccoon, or even a coyote finding it while she was away hunting, and the animal would be sure to eat her chicks.

She needed a better place, and she already knew where it would be.

Across the tall grass she flew in the darkness. Her great golden eyes saw clearly without the need of daylight. Her huge body, fully a foot and a half in height, moved through the night sky and over the far corral where the twelve palomino trail ponies stood dozing.

She circled over the sleeping llamas, lying close together as they were, and on around the barn and the large ranch house. The owl knew it was best to first circle the stable, which was her destination, and check for danger before entering. It was what she always did. She had not become a full-grown owl by taking chances.

She flew over the huge iron gate with the letters "BB" worked into them. It did not matter to her that the letters stood for "Bradford Brothers" or that the gate had weathered summers and winters for more than fifty years.

Completing her circle, she swooped into the open window of the hayloft and settled onto a rafter over the feed room. She had been here many times, and could be assured of a meal every time.

Rats and mice, and occasionally snakes, were to be found among the barrels and sacks of grain, and her chicks required their weight in food every day. This had been a very good place to hunt, and then she had noticed the dark cavity near the roof.

She knew instantly that this would make a very good nest.

The new nest would be high off the ground and would be very near to where she hunted. There was only one problem, and that problem was the many humans who came and went constantly.

At first she had watched and had not entered the stable when humans were around, but then there was the time that she had been inside and one of them came in. She was certain the human had seen her, but it had made no move to disturb her. She had waited quietly until the human had gone, and she had not come back for a while.

Then, after considering the matter, she hated to give up her good hunting place, and had begun coming back. The humans seemed to pay her no more attention than she would pay to the eagle soaring in the clouds above her.

So now that this year's chicks were gone, it was time to move her nest. The dark cave near the top of the stable was just to her liking. It was big enough, but not too big, and was closed in just enough to keep curious chicks from falling out.

She brought a few of the sticks from her old nest, but then decided new ones would be better, and she would get them later. For now, she would fly out over the canyon and down the river, and she would enjoy being free of the continuous grind of bringing food to the chicks.

After a good fly, which soothed her strong wing muscles, she returned to her new home. Huddling in the comforting dimness of the box, she napped.

Then, when she had just hopped from the small "cave" and flapped up to a rafter, ready to fly through the window of the loft, a small human stepped through the stable door.

While the owl paused, the human turned and stepped back, and the owl had taken to the air and sailed out the window of the loft. It was clear to her now that humans were not a threat to her. Maybe their eyes were weak and they couldn't even see her.

At the stable door, ten-year-old Nelda Bradford stopped and turned, holding her finger to her lips for silence. Her thirteen-year-old sister, Caitlyn, was right behind her.

"She did it!" was the excited whisper of the girl.

"Did what?" demanded her sister.

"Find the nest! Didn't you see her fly up through the loft?"

"No. I was trying to keep from running into you when you turned around in front of me! I almost stepped on your heels."

"Well, I had to stop. The owl was on the rafter by the nest box Josh put up. He said she would find it, and when she did, she would be better than a rattrap for catching the mice and things in the barn. Let's go look!"

The tall ladder was leaned against the inside of the stable, and Nelda shinnied up, faster than a monkey. "Aw, there's only a few sticks in it! Maybe she doesn't like it."

"We could ask Josh. He'll be around here somewhere."

Josh Hunt was the wrangler for the "BB" Ranch, taking care of the many horses used by guests to ride on trail rides, and also those used for renting to anybody who needed them. In addition, sometimes movies being shot on the ranch needed horses. Josh knew a lot of things about horses, and he always knew where every horse was.

The Bradford sisters had come to the stable to saddle their own horses for a ride over the meadow. Because it was so hot late in the day, they liked to ride in the early mornings.

This year had been a very hot year, and the dry wind raced over the meadows, sucking the moisture out of everything it touched. All of the state of Oklahoma had been dry, but the ranches in the Panhandle had suffered most. They were always the ones that suffered the most when there was a hot summer.

Crops of grain were stunted in their growth when the rains didn't come, and the grass dried out and seeded early, making less pasture for the animals. Far in the distance were the high-fenced pastures of the bison, their dark bodies easy to see against the light gold color of the grass.

On a guest ranch like the "BB," there was always a lot of work to be done. In the summer, there were guests who came to spend time in the cottages, and there were groups who came on field trips to see the bison, ride the horses, or just to see what a working ranch looked like.

It was good to have the guests, because these visitors were glad to pay for the privilege of staying in the cabins, and the money they paid was always needed, but it still made a lot of work for everyone.

Mom had posted the "duty rooster" before breakfast, and everyone had several things to do. Thirteen-year-old Cal, twin brother to Caitlyn, had to move the llamas to a different pasture where they could get more grass. Those shaggy animals were another good thing for the ranch, because they were very popular with children. The ones at the "BB" ranch were tame enough to pet.

During the school year, there had been several times that whole classes of school children had come to the ranch for a field trip to pet the llamas and ride the gentle trail palominos. The fees they paid were very welcome.

The duty rooster in the kitchen had told Caitlyn and Nelda they must take the small tractor and trailer to the field and bring the last of the melons into the icehouse. The guests they expected later in the day would want the melons to be icy cold. They were very popular with the guests. Then the girls would check all the cottages for soap and towels and whatever else was needed.

Work came before riding. Caitlyn turned the key in the tractor ignition, and a roar and a puff of blue smoke followed. Nelda loaded the wooden board they used as a loading ramp for the huge melons, and climbed into the trailer beside it. Mom usually reminded them, "Don't be trying to lift those big melons. You'll break your back. Roll them up the ramp, and be sure to work together on them."

So they took the ramp.

There would be at least two loads, one for the large watermelons, and the other for the very popular late cantaloupes. Nelda took the end gate off the trailer and leaned the "ramp" against it, while Caitlyn selected a melon that looked ripe.

Some of the melons were as big as three basketballs, and the girls clipped the stems from the vine and rolled them toward the trailer, then, together, they pushed them up the slanted board.

It took a little time, but they couldn't have lifted the melon if they had tried, so Mom might just as well have saved her breath!

At the turn of a key, the tractor roared into life again, and zipped out of the garden gate on its way to the icehouse. Of course, it wasn't really an icehouse, just a small cabin with very thick walls and a very powerful air conditioner in every window. It made the melons really cold.

Next, the tractor scooted around to the garden at the back of the stable where the golden cantaloupes grew. They were a lot easier to load, because they were more the size of a soccer ball, but the trailer held more of them, so it evened out.

There would also be vegetables for the girls to pick, but they could wait until evening because the green things didn't need time to cool out.

So now they had a little time to ride their ponies. They found them in the near corral, their heads hanging over the fence in anticipation.

Caitlyn's pony was called Golden, and Nelda's was Vanilla, but it would be hard for most people to tell them apart. They both had the cream colored bodies trimmed with flowing manes and tails, and they were exactly the same size.

Saddled and mounted, the ponies happily trotted through the "BB" gate and down the graveled road, their dainty hoofs clicking and grinding on the gravel of the road.

Together the girls rode in silence for a while.

"I wonder where Josh was?"

"I don't know. He has a lot to do besides answering our questions, I guess. I'll bet the owl likes the box. Josh thought she would and he's usually right."

"I know what! If she builds a nest there, then that means she's our owl, and if she's our owl then she needs a name."

"So you can teach her to come when you call her?"

"No, silly! Just that we need something to call her instead of 'the owl'."

"Well, she isn't a hoot owl, so we can't call her Hooty. She's as tall as a rooster and has those rings around her eyes like a monkey, but I don't think she would like either of those names, either."

"She's kind of whiteish with flecks of some color, as near as I could see. She almost looks like cooked oatmeal with raisins in it."

"How about 'Oatmeal'?"

"For a name? Hey, yeah! That's a good name. You know what?"

"What?"

"Remember how Josh said some early native Americans used to think an owl that flew in the daytime was up to no good, and only trying to steal the brains out of people or animals?"

"Yeah, why?"

"I just wondered if our guests might be afraid to come out of their cottages with Oatmeal around." Nelda frowned with concern.

"I wouldn't worry, kiddo," her sister reassured her. "The guests won't even know they should be afraid of anything unless someone tells them. Most of them might not even know she's an owl. Remember how we didn't know till Josh told us."

"Yeah, you're right."

"You know something? It's time to go home. Work's waiting."

"Do you know who's coming tomorrow?"

"Two grandparents bringing a little boy and girl for two days, and a girl's club of big girls is coming for the day. I think maybe there's someone else, but I don't remember who."

"How old are the girls?" Nelda was always hoping for someone her age to make friends with.

"They're too old for you. I think they're fifteen, at least."

Back under the "BB" gate and into the corral came the ponies. The girls brushed them down as was required by their father, and they stowed away the saddles. It was time for work.

It was early the next day when the van belonging to Mr. and Mrs. Sealy came down the gravel road and the two small children saw the big iron gate just ahead.

"Almost there, kids," Grandpa advised. "Look up ahead."

"It says 'BB' on the gate. Why?" asked six-year-old Billy.

When he received no answer, he offered, "I'll bet they have BB guns there that go Pop! Pop!"

Eight-year-old Cindy scoffed, "Of course not. It means Bed and Breakfast, doesn't it, Grandpa."

"Could be. They have a bed for us, and tomorrow we will eat breakfast. Sounds good enough to me."

The Sealy's were hardly settled in their cottage when the Girl's Club arrived. There were six girls of fifteen and sixteen, and they insisted they were experienced riders, and didn't need anyone along with them.

However, Josh went along anyway. He didn't trust the horses with anyone he didn't know. And he didn't trust girls he didn't know when they said they were experienced riders. Maybe they were and maybe they were not!

The girls had hardly gone a mile when they were hot and sweaty and were not having a lot of fun.

They drank their glass bottled sodas and rested in the shade, and then Josh took them down in the box canyon to the river.

They were more interested in playing in the water than riding, so he circled back to pick up the bottles they had pitched aside, and then he waited in the shade of a tree until they were ready to leave.

As they climbed up the narrow trail out of the canyon, they walked the horses single file and Josh brought up the rear. One of the girls took a last soft drink bottle from her saddlebag, and when she decided it was not cold enough, she dropped it down the side of the canyon bluff, where it rolled, end over end, almost to the valley floor. Josh was busy watching the trail at the time.

At the ranch house, Mom served ice cold cantaloupes with vanilla ice cream, topped with crumbled chocolate and nuts for the girls to eat now, and she wrapped up two dozen homemade cookies for the girls to take with them when they left.

Their driver, dozing in the shade, was aroused up from his nap to take them back to the city.

Mom had been sure that city girls would find it too hot to have fun this late in the year, but they had insisted on coming, and they came, but they left early. So it was a short, easy day for Mom and Josh and the girls were charged for a whole day so it worked out well.

Mom hoped the memory of the melon sundaes and the cookies might make the girls forget how hot and miserable they had been. They might even want to come back sometime. Maybe when it was cooler.

Old Uncle Raymond Red Hawk had entertained the Sealy grandchildren while their grandparents rested in the lawn chairs. Hot wind blew across the yard but the old couple didn't seem to mind it enough to go into the cool cottage.

All in all it was not a bad day, and Caitlyn and Nelda finally got to go to their cool room and read.

Outside the window was the sound of the tractor pulling the grass mower. Their seventeen-year-old brother, Roger, was cutting a wide swath of grass all the way around the ranch, the barn and stable, around the pens where the llamas were kept, and out around the horse corrals. Yesterday he had cut a band of grass all the way down to the bison pasture following the tall fence.

Caitlyn looked out her window as he passed by, his straw hat pushed down, and a bandana tied over his nose and mouth. *Must be a lot of wind blowing the dust around,* she decided. He looked hot and tired, but the tractor rumbled on. Work had to be done.

Circling the ranch houses with the mower could only mean one thing.... fire danger. The tall prairie grass was as crisp as tissue paper in the sun, and the fiery golden ball of sunshine beat down on it all day, scorching it even more.

The cloudless sky was as blue as a baby doll's eyes and stretched from horizon to horizon. Not good.

Even the grasshoppers that always whirred through the grass were perched on the stalks, chewing without much success on the tough leaf spears.

The horses and llamas ate grain and baled hay when there was not much grass, but the bison were not bothered by the drought. Centuries of evolution had fitted them to eat whatever was available and make it do, and they grazed on the parched grass and then lay in the hot sun to rest and chew their cuds.

Roger and the tractor disappeared in the distance and Caitlyn stared out across the grass. On a sudden impulse, she took her camera from its case and snapped a few shots out toward the canyon.

The heat reflected up in waves making the air almost appear golden. Maybe the camera could pick up the heat waves and it would make an interesting picture. Roger reappeared on the next round and Caitlyn snapped his picture as he went by.

Well, soon the sun would be down, and everything would cool off a little. Still she stood watching.

Down in the box canyon, a raccoon sniffed a strange scent, and being a nosey creature, he tracked it down. The smell seemed to be coming from a strange hard thing that was so big around it took both of his little black-fingered hands to pick it up.

Something poured out of it, flowing down his vest fur, so he put the thing down and began to lick his chest hair to clen it.

The sweet stuff tasted so good, that he again picked up the hard thing with the stuff in it, and tried to drink it, but instead, he spilled more down his fur. Bored with it all, he washed his hands with his tongue and wandered off to the river to look for crawfish.

As he stepped over the hard thing, his foot hit it and sent it spinning on down from the narrow trail toward the floor of the canyon. He paused a minute to watch it, then headed on down to the river for a snack.

A coyote loped across the valley grass and his eye caught a flash of something. He turned and saw the strange thing, and sniffed it. The unfamiliar smell of it made him sneeze, and he shook his head and walked away.

Anything that smelled that strange was surely not good to eat, so why bother with it?

A mama possum with three babies clinging to the fur of her back had watched the coyote turn aside, and if the coyote didn't want the strange thing, maybe she should see what it was. Maybe she would want to eat it. She was not very particular about what she ate.

Drawing closer, she sniffed the strange scent and twitched her nose whiskers, but a mama possum is open to eating just about anything that does not eat her first, so she took a bite, closing her sharp teeth on the small end of it.

The strange object resisted being bitten, and scooted away like a live thing. The possum followed it across the grass and bit it again, with the same result.

On closer inspection, she found a small hole in the end, and by running her tongue inside, she could taste something. She spent several minutes licking, and then all the taste was gone.

- END OF EXCERPT -

ADDITIONAL BOOK SERIES
BY JOANN KLUSMEYER

The Great I Am Bible Story Series for Kids
6 books

The Young Pioneers Adventure Series for Kids
5 books

The Wentworth Triplets Mystery Series for Young Teens
3 books

Footsteps in the Canyon Adventure Series for Young Teens
4 books

Burnt Tree Junction Historical Fiction Series for Adults
6 books

Ozark Mountains Historical Fiction Series for Adults
7 books

Taming the Wilderness Historical Fiction Series for Adults
4 books

The Sheltering Stone Historical Fiction Series for Adults
5 books

The Trilogy of Wishbone Hollow Historicial Fiction Series for Adults
3 books

www.ingramcontent.com/pod-product-compliance
Lightning Source LLC
Chambersburg PA
CBHW070604180626
46817CB00005B/1991